CLOSE CALL

Hannibal came lunging out of the weeds with the agility of a panther. He no longer had the cane knife, but before Torn could bring his own blade into play Hannibal was on him, knocking him clean out of the saddle.

Torn fell poorly and nearly blacked out. He got unsteadily to his feet and dived sideways as Hannibal, now astride Torn's horse, tried to run him down. The river pirate laughed harshly, checked the horse and turned to look back.

"You fight good!" he roared. "Someday we fight again." He shook his fist at Torn and galloped away, his crazy laughter ringing in Torn's ears.

Torn had the feeling that he was extremely lucky to be alive. Hannibal was a natural-born fighter. Strong, quick, talented—and deadly.

They would fight again, and the next time one of them wouldn't walk away.

Also by Hank Edwards

THE JUDGE

WAR CLOUDS

GUN GLORY

TEXAS FEUD

STEEL JUSTICE

LAWLESS LAND

BAD BLOOD

Published by
HARPERPAPERBACKS

HANK EDWARDS

THE JUDGE

RIVER RAID

HarperPaperbacks
A Division of HarperCollinsPublishers

This is a work of fiction. The characters, incidents, and dialogues are products of the author's imagination and are not to be construed as real. Any resemblance to actual events or persons, living or dead, is entirely coincidental.

HarperPaperbacks *A Division of* HarperCollins*Publishers*
10 East 53rd Street, New York, N.Y. 10022

Cover illustration by Bill Maughan

First printing: October 1992

Printed in the United States of America

HarperPaperbacks and colophon are trademarks of HarperCollins*Publishers*

10 9 8 7 6 5 4 3 2 1

CHAPTER 1

THE TOWN OF HARD TIMES HAD EARNED ITS NAME. ONCE IT had been a thriving community. But on the day Clay Torn arrived it looked to be, in his studied opinion, one step shy of oblivion.

The streets were all but empty. A couple of old-timers and a bored store clerk sat on split-log benches or splint-bottomed chairs in the shade of the boardwalks, snoozing under a hat brim or whittling on a shingle or reading a wildcat novel.

A sow and its litter filed across the rutted street, trailed at a cautious distance by a black-and-orange bob-tail cat.

Three young boys, barefoot and shirtless and dirty, their bony shoulders sun-blistered, were playing tag in and around an empty ramshackle clapboard. They popped in and out of doorways and glassless windows and lurked in the adjacent weed-overgrown alley.

Torn came in from the west, on a road that tailed out

1

of thick pine forest and curled through fields of corn. The crops were clearly suffering from the summer's drought. A stingy breath of wind whispered through the dry stalks.

He was leading a chestnut gelding. The horse limped, favoring its left front leg. Horse and man were covered with a thick patina of red dust. Torn's black frock coat, trousers, and boots were caked with it. His white linen shirt was damp with sweat.

A craggy white-haired man wearing overalls on top of pink underriggings sat in front of the Hard Times Hotel, his chair tilted back against the shiplap wall. When he spotted Torn, he leaned forward, bringing the chair down on all four spindly legs. Elbows on knees, gnarled hands clasped, he squinted west against the afternoon sun and watched the newcomer with rheumy pale blue eyes.

The old-timer could tell that Torn had come a "fur piece" afoot; that tall chestnut had lamed up a ways back. The man in dusty black was bone weary—the codger read this fact in the slope of Torn's shoulders and by the way Torn's head hung down. But the old-timer surmised that this one could walk forever if he had to, come hell or high water. The stranger's stride was still long and steady—no shuffling or dragging of heels here.

Hell or high water. The old-timer chuckled, a raspy sound, like a gravedigger's shovel striking deep into hard ground. Hell, maybe. But there wasn't much water, period, in these parts. Not a chance of high water around here. That was Hard Times' problem. The old-timer looked wistfully east in the direction of the old levee. Piles of wooden skids littered the slope and rim.

The Mississippi River—the "Old Man"—had once been found on the other side of that levee. But the river had changed its course, as it was wont to do. Now a hike to the top of the levee offered nothing more than a depressing view of weed-covered bottom, or boggy swamp when it rained.

It hadn't rained in a coon's age, and then some. The old-timer squinted at the sky. Big white thunderclouds had built up, like they did every afternoon, just about. They looked like they carried plenty of rain. But you couldn't prove that by a living soul in this parched country. Those clouds never spread out their tops or opened up their bellies.

The old-timer turned his attention back to the newcomer, still coming doggedly on. Beyond the stranger the cornfields were brown and withered. The old-timer shook his head, hawked, and spat phlegm.

In his years he had seen all kinds of extreme weather. He knew it would rain, eventually. When it did, it would come a real fence lifter, more than likely. The river, a mile to the east these days, would probably rise over its banks and drown a hundred people. Mother Nature never did anything in moderation. Neither did the Mississippi.

Of course the local preachers blamed it on the people and their sinning ways. They declared that the Lord Almighty was punishing His wayward flock. The old-timer was inclined to think it was the devil who had a hand in all this recent misery. Ol' Satan sure seemed to have it in for Hard Times. First he had taken the river away, and now he'd made off with the rain. One cross to bear after another, that was this town's fate.

Scratching at a grayback, the codger studied the

stranger in black. Maybe more trouble. Gambler? Lawman? Outlaw? This man was no Bible thumper. Nor whiskey drummer. Nor down-at-heels drifter either. The old-timer wasn't sure how he knew this. He just knew. Maybe it came from years of studying people coming down that very road.

Torn angled over to the hotel and nodded agreeably at the old-timer.

The old-timer nodded back. "Howdy, stranger. What happened to your cayuse?"

"Abscess under the shoe is my guess," said Torn. He took off his hat and used a sleeve to wipe sweat off his brow. "Pulled up lame yesterday."

The old-timer keenly scrutinized Torn. He saw a tall, lean man with flinty gray eyes and close-cropped hair the color of that parched corn yonder. He also saw the Colt in a holster on Torn's hip, under the long frock coat. No badge, at least not visible.

"Ol' Jube over at the livery's the man to see," said the codger. "He'll pull that iron off and soak the hoof in turpentine and wintergreen. But it'll take a few days to heal up."

"Know anybody who wants a good horse?" Torn smiled wryly. "Any reasonable offer accepted."

This one's a well-educated son, mused the old-timer. But he ain't no highfalutin dandy. A gentleman once, but there's hard bark on him now. Been through the mill, seen the elephant, and knows how to use that shooting iron, guaranteed.

"Name's Harlan Cratchett," said the old-timer, rising stiffly and sticking out a hand.

Torn shook the hand. "Glad to make your acquaintance, Mr. Cratchett."

"Reckon I better buy him from you. Don't know nobody else round these parts who'd be able to." Cratchett looked the chestnut over, running his hands over the animal's haunches and legs, checking its teeth to confirm its age, seeing in a glance with an experienced eye that the horse was sound. The abscess was a temporary problem. Its tendons were straight, its hocks weren't too far apart, its rib cage wasn't too small, its back wasn't swayed. It wasn't wind-broke, and it wasn't a stargazer.

"You'll be going on the river then?" asked Cratchett.

"Yes. St. Louis."

"The *Sultana* ought to be by here tomorrow, up from New Orleans."

Torn looked across at the desolate levee.

"Landing's a mile from here," said Cratchett. "I'll run you over in a mud wagon. I do that for my guests, free gratis, ever since the river divorced us. So far, this go-round, there's you, the old gentleman and his daughter, and a feller name of Sikes. Now, about this cayuse. How's sixty dollars sound?"

"Make it seventy-five and I'll throw in the saddle."

Cratchett tugged on an earlobe. The saddle was a good center-fire rig. Nothing fancy, but no hen skin, either.

"Okay. Reckon I can sell horse and saddle to some younker all set on going west to get scalped by Injuns. Lord knows I see a dozen ever' week, fresh off the farm. Not many prospects in this neck of the woods these days. Now, friend, I got to ask you, do you have proof this animal belongs to you all legal like? I don't mean to be rude, and I ain't looking for trouble, but you can't be too careful."

Torn's smile was tolerant. "I've got a bill of sale. Will that do?"

Cratchett was apologetic. "Like I said, I don't mean anything by the asking. You see, there's this damned bunch of no-account thieves and river pirates around here. Jack Jenkins and his men. They have a habit of selling stolen goods and then stealing them right back again. Ol' Jenkins is a wily swamp rat. He's been doing that sort of thing for nigh on thirty years. Used to be slaves. Now it's livestock mostly."

"I know about Jenkins."

Cratchett tilted his head, closed one eye, and peered at Torn through the other. "You do?"

"But I'm probably the last man on earth Jenkins would want working for him."

"Why come?"

"Because I'm a federal judge," said Torn. "And I just hanged three men believed to be part of his gang over in Bayou Sorrel."

"That news makes me glad and sorry at the same time."

"How's that?"

"Well, I'm right glad three of them two-legged rats is dead," declared Cratchett, "and sorry as hell for you, Judge, if Jack Jenkins catches you."

CHAPTER

2

HARLAN CRATCHETT OFFERED TORN THE BEST ROOM IN THE hotel, no charge. Torn insisted, firmly but politely, on paying. He thought that had there been enough people left in Hard Times to make up one, Cratchett would have organized a parade on his behalf.

The best room in the house wasn't much, but it was better than many Torn had seen in his frontier travels. A narrow iron bed, sagging in the middle, a chest of drawers with white paint peeling badly in the bayou-country humidity, a suspicious-looking straight-back chair he dared not sit on. The room was upstairs, overlooking the street.

Cratchett brought him fresh water in a jug, and Torn poured some in a chipped porcelain bowl on the small chest of drawers. Stripping off his coat, he unstrapped the shoulder harness that held, tight against his rib cage and upside down beneath his left arm, his leather-sheathed saber-knife. This he put on the bed, next to his

Winchester 44/40 long gun. Removing his shirt, he washed his face, arms, neck, and upper body. Finding a razor and mirror in his black leather valise, he scraped the beard stubble off his face, propping the mirror against the splashboard of the chest of drawers.

A little while later Cratchett returned to inform him that supper would be served downstairs in the kitchen in an hour.

"My wife was the best cook in the parish. She run off with a Missouri horse trader." He pronounced Missouri "misery." "Acadian, she was, and my vittles don't hold a candle to hers, but I'm afraid you won't find an honest-to-goodness restaurant in this town no more. Caught up a mess of catfish this morning. Hope that suits you, Judge. If not, you just tell me what you're hankering for and I'll—"

"That'll suit me fine," said Torn.

"Well, if there's anything else . . ."

"Just sleep."

"You just go right on. I'll see to it you ain't disturbed."

Torn thanked him, locked the door, and stretched his weary bones out on the bed.

As tired as he was, sleep eluded him. Every time he closed his eyes and began to doze, he saw three men on a gallows, hoods over their heads, rope around their necks. And then the trapdoors would spring open and the three men dropped—and Torn would snap wide-awake with the sensation of choking.

For ten years now he had been a frontier judge, assigned to the Tenth Circuit out of St. Louis. In that stretch of time he had presided over hundreds of trials, had sentenced dozens of criminals to death.

But he just couldn't get used to the executions.

It wasn't that the men he sentenced to die hadn't deserved their fate. The trio hanged last week in Bayou Sorrel certainly had. They had stolen a horse, sold it to a farmer, and the very next night had attempted to steal it back. The farmer had surprised them. They had killed him. The trial had taken less than an hour, the jury less than a minute to reach a verdict of guilty. Torn's sentence, under the circumstances, had been fit and proper.

Still, it bothered him.

He believed that every man, no matter how despicable a character, deserved a fighting chance. Which was precisely why he so often took upon himself the role of jury and executioner.

In the opinions of many this penchant for taking the law into his own hands was wrong. For every man he had sentenced to the gallows he had slain two with knife or gun. More than one newspaper and politician and fine, upstanding private citizen had branded him a cold-blooded killer.

Torn didn't see it that way. In his mind there was nothing more cold-blooded than a hanging. At least the men he brought to justice on his own, without benefit of trial by jury, had had a fair chance in a fair fight. Sure, it violated the tenet that every man deserved to be judged by a jury of his peers, but Torn's conscience was clear.

His rather old-fashioned concept of fair play stemmed from his upbringing as the blue-blood son of a South Carolina planter. Torn had been reared a gentleman. But the War Between the States had radically altered the course of his life. A Confederate cavalry officer, he had been wounded and captured at Gettysburg, and condemned to sixteen months of living hell in a federal prisoner-of-war camp. Escaping in the last days of the war, he had returned to South Carolina to find his home destroyed by bluecoat invaders, his family all dead, and his fiancée, Melony Hancock, vanished without trace.

Rumor had it that Yankee deserters had abducted Melony and headed west, and it was west Torn had gone in search of her. Now, ten long years later, he was still searching. He carried a photograph of her—a daguerreotype. Everywhere he went he showed it to people; in ten years he calculated he'd asked ten thousand people if they had ever seen her. The result: a few false leads, and daily disappointment. But he didn't give up. He didn't know how to give up.

In spite of the long and lonely years of futile searching, his love for Melony burned as strongly as ever. The job he held was simply a means to an end, and the end was finding her, and putting the pieces of a life shattered by the war back together again. A federal judge traveled far and wide: the Tenth Circuit stretched from the Dakotas to the Mississippi delta country. A big territory, and Torn couldn't help but believe that somewhere there was someone who knew something about his lost love.

The fact that an ex-Confederate served as a federal judge was a bone of contention for many. After all, they argued, Torn had killed a Union sergeant during his escape from Maryland's Point Lookout prison camp. The fact that the sergeant had been a sadistic son of a bitch was not, for them, sufficiently mitigating to absolve Torn. Yet Torn had been absolved. His prewar study of the law at the University of Virginia had stood him in good stead. In the spirit of reconciliation that had been the major theme of his administration, President

Andrew Johnson had appointed Torn to one of the most difficult and dangerous jobs on the frontier.

And few could deny that he had done the job well. He had become something of a living legend, admired by some, hated by others, and feared by almost every outlaw from the Absaroka to the Atchafalaya.

The saber-knife he carried was an integral part of that legend. It had once been a Chicopee saber, the property of the sadistic Point Lookout sergeant. Torn had used it to kill the man. When the blade broke, he'd honed what was left down to its present fifteen inches of razor-sharp tempered steel. He wore it concealed under his coat, a deadly ace-in-the-hole.

While he conceded that the saber-knife had proven useful over the years, Torn had no fondness for it. It was an ugly reminder of an ugly past. But he could no more part with it than he could the daguerreotype of Melony Hancock.

CHAPTER

3

GIVING UP ON SLEEP, TORN ROSE, FOUND A CLEAN SHIRT IN HIS valise, and put it on. He tried to brush some of the dirt out of his black frock coat, with marginal success. He thought he might do better hiking down to the landing and plunging, clothes and all, into the Mississippi.

Strapping on the saber-knife and his Colt sidegun, a .45 Peacemaker, he gathered up his hat and stepped out into the upstairs hallway. A whiff of fresh-brewed coffee triggered his appetite and reminded him that he hadn't enjoyed a decent meal in days.

As he passed the door at the top of the staircase, it opened suddenly and a man stumbled out, a hand over his face.

Torn's first thought was that the man was injured. Then the fragrance of gin told him otherwise. The man wasn't watching where he was going and collided with Torn. The impact threw Torn off balance, jamming him against the flimsy banister, almost spilling him down the stairs. Torn's aggressive reaction was pure reflex. He pushed off the banister with shoulder lowered and drove the man back against the wall.

With an incoherent snarl of rage and surprise the man threw a clumsy haymaker. Torn had already danced back out of range. He gave his opponent a split-second once-over, sizing him up. The man was a burly character, thick through the chest and shoulders, with unruly hair the color of rust on iron, and small eyes so dark brown they looked black. He wore moleskin pants tucked into mule-ear boots. An Arkansas Toothpick was stuck into one of the boots as well. The man opted to leave the knife where it was and grabbed for the Navy Colt stuck in his belt.

Before the Navy Colt came clear, Torn had his Peace-maker drawn, cocked, and aimed.

The man froze.

"I don't ordinarily draw iron without using it," said Torn. "But I'm trying to take into account that you're stinking drunk, and nothing makes a fool out of a man faster than a bottle of cheap tongue oil."

For one breathless moment the man teetered on the brink of a fatal mistake. But Torn's fierce calm shook him, and he lost confidence in himself. He took his hand off the Navy Colt. Blushing from the shame of it, and sensing, correctly, that there was no danger of Torn pulling the trigger as long as he left his own gun alone, the man mustered up some bravado in an attempt to repair his damaged ego.

"You sayin' I'm a fool?"

"If the shoe fits."

"Why don't you watch where you're going? Knock me down the stairs next time."

Torn's smile was pure ice as he holstered the Colt Peacemaker.

"I'll give it some thought."

Prudent enough to refrain from more inflammatory talk, the man brushed past Torn and clumped heavily down the stairs.

"Smart pilgrims who enjoy breathing stay out of my way," he muttered belligerently without looking back.

Exhibiting prudence of his own, Torn managed to resist laughing at this tough talk. He had heard this song a hundred times before. Loud talkers didn't worry him. He knew it was the men who let their actions speak for them that you had to watch out for.

He was about to follow the man down when a whisper of sound in the hallway behind him made him turn.

There were four upstairs rooms in Cratchett's hotel. Torn and the man with whom he had just locked horns occupied the two rooms on the north side. A young woman stood in the doorway of the room directly across from Torn's.

She was a breathtaking beauty. Her hair, bound up with amber pins, was the color of white gold. Her eyes were gray, of a much lighter and more delicate shade than Torn's. Her mouth was small, the lips full and ruby red. Her complexion was peaches and cream. She wore a dark blue serge dress and matching basque. She had the bearing of a highborn lady, and Torn reacted by sweeping the hat from his head.

"I didn't realize you were there, ma'am," he said. "I apologize for the unpleasantness."

She smiled, her eyes sparkling. "I am highly pleased that you did not shoot him, sir. The sight of blood would have surely spoiled my appetite."

Torn was mesmerized. She looked and dressed like a gentlewoman, but there was a touch of the brazen in her smile, and more than a trace of audacity in her bold gaze. Somehow he doubted that bloodshed would have sent her scrambling for the smelling salts.

In some respects she reminded him of Melony. She didn't look at all like his fiancée; Melony's hair had been as black as a raven's wing, her eyes the deep blue of a twilight summer sky. But Melony, while she had tried to always act the way a proper young Southern lady should, had been more than a little headstrong and mischievous. This young woman struck Torn as being cut from the same cloth.

"I'm relieved to know I did not cause you any distress, ma'am," he replied, a little tongue-in-cheek.

She laughed discreetly, but the laughter died, to be replaced by a carefully arranged impassivity as the door to the fourth room opened and a white-haired gentleman in a white summer suit appeared.

"What is it, Rebecca? What are you up to now, child?"

"Nothing, Father. I—"

The man peered suspiciously at Torn. "Who are you, sir, and what business do you have with my daughter?"

CHAPTER 4

"FATHER!"

The white-haired man ignored his daughter's protest. "Well, sir? A gentleman does not speak to a lady before he has been properly introduced."

"The name's Torn. Clay Torn. And if my manners are a little rusty, it's because I haven't been in very polite company of late."

"Torn? Torn." The man pulled on the neatly trimmed goatee adorning his chin. Bushy white brows knit, he contemplated the ceiling. "By heaven, man, the name rings a bell. I can't quite . . . wait! Of course! Andrew Jackson Torn, of South Carolina. Would you be . . . ?"

"His son."

The man leaped forward to shake Torn's hand.

"By heaven, yes! Why, I knew you as a child. Perhaps you remember me? John Raleigh Ashbrook, at your service. My lands, boy, your father and I were old friends."

16

"I'm afraid I don't remember you," said Torn, "but I'm pleased to make your acquaintance."

"Well, no matter!" boomed Ashbrook, effusive. "As I say, you were quite young when last we met. A great deal of water under the bridge since then. But what a happy coincidence to meet you once more, after so many years. Whoever coined the phrase 'it's a small world' certainly knew whereof he spoke. What brings you here? You wouldn't be going on the river, by any chance?"

"As a matter of fact I am. Up to St. Louis."

"What a wonderful development! So are we. Oh, I beg your pardon. I have been remiss. Allow me to introduce my daughter, Rebecca. My dear, this is Clay Torn, the son of my old friend Andrew Torn. You remember, I'm sure, my speaking of Andrew Torn."

"Yes, Father."

Torn detected a trace of diffidence in her answer and noticed that now she avoided his gaze. This wasn't shyness, but rather embarrassment. Something was bothering her. Was it the way her father was carrying on? Or something more?

In truth there was something about John Raleigh Ashbrook that didn't quite ring true—something Torn couldn't quite put his finger on. He had no idea if this man had in fact been a friend of his father's. Andrew Torn had had many friends and acquaintances. A fair-minded, sociable man, he had been well liked by almost everyone fortunate enough to know him.

Still, there was something in Ashbrook's hail-fellow-well-met bonhomie that put Torn on his guard.

"Your father," said Ashbrook. "How is he, may I ask?"

"He's dead."

Ashbrook was shocked. "Dear God in heaven! When? How?"

"At the end of the war. A heart attack."

Torn thought it odd that Ashbrook didn't know—if indeed he had been such a close personal friend of Andrew Jackson Torn. But to put the question bluntly would have been discourteous.

Ashbrook saved him the trouble. "You must forgive me for my ignorance, and for causing you any pain by posing the question. But you see, I left Louisiana in sixty-three. Sailed to Mexico and sought refuge there. My plantation had been taken over by federal soldiers. New Orleans had fallen to the Yankees. I could not abide that ogre Butler. Calling my slaves contraband! Confiscating my cotton! I have only recently returned."

"No need to apologize," said Torn, his suspicions somewhat allayed. Ashbrook's explanation seemed reasonable. Quite a few Southerners, planters and soldiers and politicians, had chosen flight to Latin America over subjugation by federal authority. In recent years some had begun to drift back to their homeland, now that the inequities—and the iniquities—of the occupation and reconstruction were things of the past.

"Rebecca's mother died our first year in Mexico," said Ashbrook, grief pulling at his features. He recovered bravely. "For quite a few years it was a struggle for my daughter and me."

"I'm sorry to hear that."

"I had taken a little money to Mexico with me. A few family heirlooms as well. What little the Yankees hadn't stolen. Finally our fortunes took a turn for the better. I had purchased some land on the coast, near Vera Cruz. Tried to raise tobacco and cotton, with little success.

Then we discovered silver on our property. I am on my way to St. Louis to meet with potential investors."

Tugging on his goatee, Ashbrook appeared to give Torn a shrewd appraisal. "A thought just struck me, my friend. I don't suppose you would be interested in a good, solid investment? There is a fortune to be made. All I need is capital, to purchase machinery, to hire the laborers. I am willing to offer a total of seventy-five percent of the profits for those wise enough to invest in the venture."

"I'm afraid I . . ."

Torn was about to inform Ashbrook that he had no money to invest. His judgeship paid two dollars a day, and he saved virtually none of it. He had to pay all his expenses from that wage.

But he thought twice about being so candid. Apparently Ashbrook believed he was still in possession of what had once been vast family holdings. The truth of the matter was that all had been lost in the war. Ravenoak, the Torn estate, had been reduced to a pile of charred rubble by Sherman's bluecoat scavengers, and the land had been stolen by carpetbaggers.

Torn found his suspicions concerning John Raleigh Ashbrook renewed. The frontier was full to the rafters with smooth-talking confidence men. In his travels Torn had crossed paths with quite a few of that breed. He had dispatched some of them to prison. He'd heard a lot of spiels, a lot of phony get-rich-quick schemes, and Ashbrook's Mexican silver mine fit nicely into that mold.

He had no concrete evidence, and was aware that he could be doing Ashbrook a gross disservice, but he decided it would do no harm to play it close to the vest for the time being.

"I'm afraid I would have to see some documentation, Mr. Ashbrook, before I could give you an answer. I hope you understand."

"Of course, of course." Ashbrook chuckled, looking positively paternal. "It would be foolish of you not to, and I know Andrew would not have raised a fool. I have a prospectus. Assay reports. Even samples, which potential investors are free to have assayed for themselves. Perhaps after dinner we could talk further."

"Fine." Turning to Rebecca, Torn said, "I would be pleased to have the honor of escorting you to dinner, Miss Ashbrook."

"Thank you, sir," she said, with cool formality, "but it seems I have lost my appetite after all. If you will excuse me."

She returned to her room and closed the door firmly behind her.

Ashbrook was horrified. "My apologies, Clay. My daughter is a rather frail creature. Perhaps I should look in on her."

Torn nodded and started down the stairs. Ashbrook knocked on Rebecca's door and entered without waiting for an invitation. Pausing halfway down the staircase, Torn eavesdropped a moment. He heard Ashbrook speak in a low, scolding tone of voice, but he couldn't make out the words. He didn't feel the need to.

Convinced that all was not as it should be with the Ashbrooks, he sought out Cratchett and elicited a promise from the old-timer to make no mention of the fact that he was a federal judge.

Despite his aversion to hangings Torn had decided to give Ashbrook a little rope.

CHAPTER

5

"THE RIVER'S AS FICKLE AS A WOMAN," DECLARED CRATCHETT, sitting at the dinner table with Torn, Ashbrook, and the man with whom Torn had had the altercation at the top of the hotel stairs. Torn recalled Cratchett referring to this guest by the name of Sikes.

"We used to have her at the back door," continued the old-timer. "Now you have to travel a mile or so to have anything to do with her."

"I remember reading," said Ashbrook, "that the entire twelve hundred miles of the Mississippi which La Salle explored two hundred years ago is all dry land now."

Cratchett nodded, finished off the last of his grits, and slugged down some coffee, which, in Torn's opinion, had been made with Mississippi bottom slime.

"That's gospel, I reckon. Take the town of Delta. Used to be a couple miles downriver from Vicksburg. The Mississippi changed course, cut through a neck of bottomland, and lo and behold, these days Delta is a couple miles *above* Vicksburg.

"But to my way of thinkin', Delta had it easy compared to Hard Times. Not that this is the only town left high and dry by the river. Whoever come up with the handle of Hard Times must've been a gol-durned prophet. Why, a friend of mine, a farmer, went to bed one night in Louisiana and woke up next morning in Mississippi. That's why I say the river's like a woman. The man who banks on her staying put is a gold-plated dunce. Anybody want more crank?"

"Good Lord, no," said Torn.

Cratchett grinned. "Then maybe some 'shine will suit you better."

"Now you're talking," said Sikes.

Cratchett fetched a jug and poured Sikes a generous dollop in a tin cup. "You never said what you do for a living, Mr. Sikes."

"No, I didn't. You got some strong reason for wanting to know, old-timer?"

"Just curious." Unruffled, Cratchett moved around the table. Torn accepted an after-dinner dose of white lightning. Ashbrook declined and produced a silver flask with an ornately scrolled cap.

"I prefer bonded, thank you."

"Right sorry to hear your daughter's under the weather, Mr. Ashbrook," said Cratchett. "Reckon I could fix up a plate of vittles and take it to her room."

"I'll take it," said Sikes, leering. "My pa always said to do for others. That way they'll do for you."

Ashbrook stared across the table. "I don't believe I care for your manner, sir."

Sikes knocked back the moonshine and struck the

table with the empty cup. Rising out of his chair, he planted his fists on the tabletop and leaned forward belligerently.

"You picking a quarrel with me?"

"Sit down and shut up," said Torn.

Sikes glared. Torn glared right back at him. A tense moment later Sikes blinked and looked away. Petulant, he sat down.

"You wouldn't happen to know Jack Jenkins, would you, Mr. Sikes?" asked Cratchett.

The casual query gave Sikes a start. "Huh? What do you mean? I . . . of course not. What makes you ask such a fool question?"

Having observed Sikes's reaction with keen interest, Torn glanced at Cratchett, wondering why the old-timer had brought up the subject of Jenkins. Did he know, or suspect, something about Sikes?

Cratchett shrugged, indifferent. "I reckon it was a fool question," he allowed. "Just curious about my guests. Bad habit, I reckon. But since you were so all-fired reluctant to tell us what you did for a living, well . . ."

"I'll be damned," said Sikes, and laughed, or tried to. The laugh rang false. Sikes tried to appear nonchalant, but was in fact nonplussed. "You old coot, with all your years I'd've thought you'd know better than to stick your nose into other folks' business. I'd say you're too curious for your own good."

Cratchett nodded. "Right likely."

Torn wanted to stay on the subject of Jenkins, and when it appeared Cratchett was going to let Sikes off the hook, he spoke up. "What do you know about Jenkins, Mr. Cratchett?"

"More than I want to know. Folks talk about Jesse James and the Younger boys north of here, up Missouri way, like they was great shakes, but everybody along the river knows those fellers don't hold a slim candle to Jack Jenkins. I reckon sayin' Jenkins is the most bold and brutal rascal this country ever laid eyes on would be what you'd call an understatement.

"It's said he used to be a preacher. I don't know if that part's true, but he's more the devil's right-hand man than a servant of God Almighty. He's a master of disguise. When he travels, he sometimes makes out like a Bible thumper. He knows his Scripture backward and forward, and he's broken every rule in the Good Book.

"Most outlaws, if they don't work alone, roam in small bunches. But Jenkins has about five, six hundred men who do his bidding. Every flavor of cutthroat and scoundrel you could imagine. Horse thieves, counterfeiters, bootleggers, murderers, you name it. They call themselves 'strikers.' Jenkins and a handful of handpicked men sit on a council and do all the planning. The strikers carry the plans out. Jenkins is the mastermind. The others do his will. They run all the risks. He don't get his hands dirty anymore, and the law never has been able to prove a thing against him."

Cratchett helped himself to more 'shine. "That ain't to say Jenkins is scared. He ain't afraid of nothing. If one of the strikers gets out of line, Jenkins is the man to take him down a notch. They say there ain't a man alive who can whup him—fists, knives, or pistols. And God have mercy on the striker who breaks the oath."

"What oath is that?" asked Ashbrook.

"Every man in Jenkins's gang must swear an oath of allegiance to Jenkins himself. He also swears never to betray the gang, or any one member of it, even to save his own life. A few did so anyway, and every one of them died a violent death, or just vanished off the face of the earth. Jenkins's favorite method of execution is tying heavy stones to a man's ankles and dropping him, alive, into the river."

"Good heavens," breathed Ashbrook, turning very pale. "That's . . . that's uncivilized."

"That's Jenkins. But bad to the bone as he is, they tell me he is a very likable fellow. Well educated. A smooth talker. A real leader of men. I reckon he'd have to be, to keep five hundred scoundrels under his thumb."

"How did he get his start?" asked Torn.

"It was before the war. I've heard he would go into a town and carry on like a preacher. While he kept the folks spellbound with fire and brimstone like you never heard, his confederates would steal all the horses they could get their ropes on. Then they started stealing slaves. They'd talk a slave into running away, telling him they'd sell him to another planter in another state, then help him escape from his new master and split the take with him. They'd do it, too, all except the last part, about splitting the proceeds. When it came time for the reckoning, they'd murder the poor devil and dump his corpse into the Mississippi. Lord only knows how many men Jenkins has sent to the bottom of the river. Reckon that's why they call him the Corpse Maker."

"I can scarcely believe a gang so large has escaped the long arm of the law for so many years," said Ashbrook.

"Oh, the law knows where Jenkins is," said Cratchett. "He has a base of operations up in the Arkansas canebrakes. A town, really. A town filled with nothing but robbers. Population's well over a thousand, if you count the women and children. Yep, they're breeding a whole new generation of scoundrels up there.

"Right after the war the army sent in a couple companies of battle-tested infantry to clean Jenkins out. They got massacred in them canebrakes. The next time the army tried to go in by riverboat. They found the town abandoned. Jenkins and his people just disappeared into the canebrakes. The army burned the town to the ground. A few months later it was rebuilt. The army hasn't tried since. Just a waste of time, the way they see it."

"You're saying there's no stopping this man Jenkins?" asked Ashbrook.

Cratchett shrugged. "Only way to kill this snake is to chop off the head." He glanced at Torn. "Ain't been a man come along yet who could handle Jenkins. In my opinion Jack Jenkins will answer for his crimes just once, and that's on Judgment Day."

CHAPTER 6

"YOU SAID WE'D START OUT FOR THE LANDING EARLY," SAID Sikes, rising. "Reckon I'll turn in."

"Yep," said Cratchett. "Can't say for certain when the *Sultana* will be along, but it should be before noon."

Sikes left the room, and Torn heard him plodding up the stairs. He wondered if the man intended to make a nuisance of himself with Rebecca Ashbrook—and then wondered why he was feeling so protective toward the young woman. After all, if his hunch about John Ashbrook was correct, it was likely that Rebecca was a willing accomplice. Conceivably she might not even be his daughter.

In spite of this he found himself attracted to Rebecca. That in itself was disturbing. All these years he had tried to remain faithful to Melony Hancock. He hadn't always succeeded. He was only human. At times he had faltered in his determination to carry on the search for his fiancée. At times he had been weak. Every now and then he had found himself on the verge of giving up altogether.

There had been a few women along his back trail who had loved him. In most cases he had been able to resist the temptation, and their love had gone unrequited. It was a testament to the moral strength of the man that he had moved on, choosing loneliness over being unfair. For Torn had known that until he learned the truth about Melony's fate he could never give his whole heart to another woman.

But the temptations kept coming, and Rebecca Ashbrook was going to be another one—he knew that for a fact. Aware that his feelings for her—still unsorted— might color his judgment, he begged off when Ashbrook asked if he were ready to see the documentation on the Mexican silver mine. Torn used the excuse that he had had a long journey and was looking forward to a good night's rest, although he suspected he would not get much rest this night.

"I quite understand," said Ashbrook. "We'll have plenty of time on the *Sultana.* It will take all of two days to reach St. Louis." He glanced at Cratchett. "Is that not so?"

"At least. The river's mighty low."

Torn was curious to know what Ashbrook was doing in Hard Times, waiting for a riverboat, in the first place, when he could have taken passage directly from New Orleans. But he didn't air the question, fearing it might alert Ashbrook to his suspicions. Besides, he had a hunch a smooth talker like John Raleigh Ashbrook would come up with a perfectly plausible explanation.

Back in his room Torn stretched out on the bed and tried to sleep, but once again sleep eluded him. He got up and paced, restless and troubled. Occasionally he paused at the window to check the darkened street. Twice he stepped out into the upstairs hall. He could see a strip of lamplight beneath Rebecca's door, directly across from his. The room occupied by Sikes, next door, appeared to be dark. The Hard Times Hotel was quiet.

But he had a premonition that something was about to happen. That trouble was coming hell-for-leather straight at him. He had learned to trust his instincts. Five years of war and ten years on the frontier in a dangerous occupation had given him very good instincts.

After an hour of walking the floor, he settled his weary bones into a chair situated near the window so that he could turn his head one way and look down at the street, or the other and see across the hall—he'd left his own door open—to Rebecca Ashbrook's room. He waited in darkness, his weapons within easy reach.

It was close to midnight by his Ingersoll stemwinder when a brief flare of light drew his attention to the street. At first he thought his tired eyes were playing tricks on him. The street was shrouded in darkness. Then he saw it again—someone was striking a match, over there in the alley between two buildings across the street from the hotel. The end of the lighted cigarette was a speck of glowing orange in the black shadows.

Torn's pulse quickened. Something was afoot. Someone was lurking in that alley. At this hour there could be little doubt that whoever it was down there was up to no good.

Intent as a cat, Torn leaned forward and watched. His room was dark; he knew he couldn't be seen. Several times he saw the orange tip of the cigarette brighten as the man hidden in the alley took a drag. What was he waiting for? The answer soon presented itself. Torn heard a door open in the upstairs hall. He glanced that way. It wasn't Rebecca Ashbrook's door. Her light had just gone out. A floorboard creaked. Rising, Torn moved silently to his own doorway and peered around the corner, in time to see Sikes descend the stairs.

Working fast, Torn strapped on his saber-knife shoulder rig and his gunbelt. He donned the black frock coat and buttoned it up. Looking out the window once more, he saw Sikes hurry across the street and disappear into the shadows of the alley. The orange tip of the cigarette sailed through the air and disintegrated into a shower of embers as the man who had been waiting flicked the spent quirly away.

Hastening downstairs, Torn opted to go out the back way and circle around. If Sikes and the other man were holding their midnight meeting in the alley, they could not fail to see him emerge from the hotel's front entrance.

Once outside, Torn headed east, going behind several of the buildings facing the street before cutting through an alley and crossing the street more than a hundred feet from the hotel. Down another alley he reached a weed-overgrown field behind the row of structures on the north side of Hard Times's one and only thoroughfare.

Out in the middle of the field was a derelict shack, and he distinguished the shapes of two horses tied up at its rear. The windows were boarded up, but lantern light leaked through the cracks in the board-and-batten walls.

So not one, but two men had come to meet with Sikes. Torn could not be sure of the location of any one of the

three. He had to take a chance and hope that all three
were now inside the shack.

Moving with the stealth of an Apache, crouched low
in the waist-high weeds, he crossed the field, Colt
Peacemaker in hand. There was no moon, and the starlight seemed only to deepen the night shadows. Drawing closer, he heard voices pitched low, coming from
inside the shanty.

One of the horses whickered softly as Torn ap-
proached. The conversation inside was abruptly cur-
tailed. Torn froze in his tracks. A door creaked on rusty
hinges. A man stepped out onto a ramshackle porch,
silhouetted against the lantern light. Holding his breath,
Torn dropped to one knee. The weeds were high
enough to conceal him. He waited until the man returned inside, then circled to come in on the side opposite of where the horses were tethered.

There had been a window on this side of the shack.
Boards had been nailed haphazardly across it. Torn
could see inside through a space between two of them.
A lantern, on the floor, burned bright, illuminating the
three men inside the shack.

One was Sikes. Torn had never seen the other two,
but a single glance was all he needed to know they were
desperate characters.

A mulatto was leaning against the far wall, smoking a
cigarette and taking no part in the conversation between
Sikes and the third man. The mulatto had a distinctly
piratical look to him. A red kerchief was tied over his
close-cropped hair and knotted in back. He wore a
leather vest, and massive arms were crossed over a
muscular chest.

The third man was swarthy and heavyset, with black

hair and beard and a lazy eye. A pistol and a bone-handled knife were stuck under his belt.

"So you come all this way to tell me it's going to happen," said Sikes, "but you can't tell me when and where? What are you trying to pull, Blacky?"

"You don't need to know when and where," said Blacky. "You just be ready. All you have to do is get to the pilothouse and take care of the pilot. Think you can handle that, Sikes?"

Sikes didn't care for Blacky's tone of voice. "Don't worry about me. I'll do my part. Long as I get my share."

"There'll be plenty of loot to go around. The *Sultana* is a damned floating palace. Fanciest boat on the river. We'll pick the passengers clean and take everything else that ain't nailed down."

"What do we do with the passengers and the boat?"

Blacky grinned. "Bottom of the river, hoss. Ain't that the way Jenkins always does things?"

Torn couldn't believe his ears. These men were planning to waylay the *Sultana*! In the same way that road agents held up stagecoaches, they were scheming to rob a steamboat. It was incredible.

"If we pull it off," said Sikes, "it'll be the crime of the century. We'll be famous."

"I don't know about that, but we'll sure as hell be rich," said Blacky. "There ain't no if about it, though. Jenkins planned it all out himself, and when has he ever planned something that didn't work?"

"We'll have the whole United States Army on our butts," muttered the mulatto.

"You ain't scared, are you, Hannibal?" Sikes laughed.

Hannibal glared, and Sikes stopped laughing.

"Who cares about the army?" scoffed Blacky. "We handled them soldier boys before, didn't we? Besides, we're gonna kill the boat and all the witnesses. Folks'll just chalk it up to another wreck on the river. Happens all the time. Won't be nobody left alive to say otherwise."

"No survivors," said Sikes.

CHAPTER

7

"Anybody getting on the boat with you tomorrow?" Blacky asked Sikes.

"Three others. An old man who looks like old money. His pockets'll be worth picking. And he's got a daughter. I aim to do more than pick her pockets, I can tell you."

Blacky stabbed him in the chest with a blunt finger. "You won't do nothin' to draw attention to yourself, Sikes. You understand? Leave the woman alone."

"What about after we take over the *Sultana*?"

Blacky shook his head emphatically. "Won't be time for dallyin' with she-stuff. You'll just have to wait until we get back to camp. Plenty of whores there who'll see to your needs."

"I'm tired of whores," complained Sikes. "I want me a real lady for a change."

Blacky laughed in his face. "You wouldn't know what to do with a real lady, hoss."

The way Sikes leered made Torn's blood boil. "The hell I don't."

"Forget it, Sikes," advised Blacky. "You scotch this up and Jenkins'll cut you into little pieces and use you for gator bait. You've got to keep the *Sultana's* pilot from steaming away from us when we move in."

"How many men will board her."

"Fifty of us. Jenkins figures that's enough to handle the *Sultana's* crew and any of the passengers who make the mistake of trying to be heroes. We'll be in small boats, and it'll be at night, and with any luck we won't be seen until it's too late, but if we are, and you hear the alarm, you get your butt up to the pilothouse and make damn sure the *Sultana* doesn't pull away before we get aboard her."

Sikes nodded. "I know what I'm supposed to do. You done told me enough times."

"Just want to make sure the message gets through that thick skull of yours."

"Jenkins handpicked me, Blacky," reminded Sikes, offended.

"Because you were a pilot once, and that's the only reason," snapped Blacky, who obviously didn't hold Sikes in very high regard.

"There's another passenger at the hotel," said Sikes. "Tall sonuvabitch in black. He's one who'll put up a fight."

"Who is he?"

"Don't know. But he thinks high of himself. I won't mind seeing him taken down a few notches. I'd do it myself right now except, like you said, I don't want to make no trouble and draw attention to myself."

Torn realized that his request of Cratchett to keep the

fact that he was a federal judge from John Ashbrook had paid unexpected dividends. Had Sikes been aware of his identity, it would have been the first matter on the agenda of this clandestine meeting, and all three strikers would have been on their guard.

He realized as well that he had to act swiftly. If he could arrest this trio, then it was likely that Jenkins would forget about trying to waylay the *Sultana,* on the supposition that without the element of surprise his audacious scheme could not hope to succeed.

Torn had no other option available to him. He had no one to turn to for help. He had to take these three into custody by himself. There could be no delay, and he could not afford to fail. The lives of the crew and passengers of the *Sultana* were hanging in the balance.

"Don't worry about that pilgrim," Blacky advised Sikes. "We'll fill him full of lead and feed him to the fishes. Now, unless you got any more questions about what you have to do, we'll break up this shindig."

"You can stop worrying about me, damn it," said Sikes, with asperity.

"Oh, I ain't worried," replied Blacky. "You know what happens when a striker fails to do what's asked of him. I reckon you'll do it, or die."

Moving with stealth, Torn carefully worked his way around to the front of the shack. He knew he had to catch them before they extinguished the lantern, as they would before leaving.

In spite of his caution he wasn't careful enough. As he stepped up onto the porch of the shanty, a rotted plank gave way under his weight.

The crack of splintering wood was quickly followed by a volley of curses from the strikers inside. Glass shattered and the lantern light went out. Pistols barked. Hot lead pierced the thin, weathered boards of the shanty wall.

Torn threw himself to the floor of the porch. The door cracked back on its hinges. One of the strikers tripped over Torn as he charged out of the shanty. As the man lost his balance and fell his pistol discharged very close to Torn's head. Torn flinched at wood shrapnel as the bullet perforated the planking inches from his face. He rolled over on his back, sat up, and fired at virtually point-blank range into the striker. Gunflash revealed to him that the striker was the one called Blacky.

Blacky grunted and tried to rise. Torn fired again, and Blacky collapsed. Torn then turned the Colt toward the doorway and sent two more bullets into the pitch-black womb of the shanty. Muzzleflash exploded the darkness as the strikers still inside responded. Torn rolled away and got to his feet, and as he did the two strikers, Sikes and Hannibal, burst through the door, guns blazing. In such close combat Torn was astonished that he wasn't hit.

Sikes veered one way and Hannibal the other. It was Sikes who collided with Torn. The impact hurled Torn backward into a porch upright, and the upright cracked and gave way. With a rending crash the porch roof came down. The collision carried Torn and Sikes out of the reach of the collapse.

Torn lost his grip on the Colt Peacemaker. A glancing blow to the face stunned him. Tasting blood, he struck back with a vengeance. He kneed Sikes in the side and hammered a forearm across the man's neck at the same time. The blows rocked the striker sideways. Torn rolled with him, straddled him, and pounded at his face with both fists, a quick and furious flurry of blows. He felt Sikes's body go slack as he lost consciousness. Getting to his feet and stumbling away, Torn felt hot, slick blood on his hands.

The horses on the other side of the shanty were acting up, and Torn, throwing a quick look around, discovered that Hannibal had disappeared. He broke into a run. As he charged around the corner of the shack all he could make out were shapes moving in shadows, but he could see enough to realize that the third striker was mounting up. Apparently he had escaped unscathed the collapse of the porch roof.

Having lost the Colt Peacemaker, Torn reached for the saber-knife. He had buttoned up his frock coat, lest his white shirt give him away in the darkness, so now he lost precious seconds in undoing the coat in order to reach the saber-knife.

It occurred to him that a rational man in this situation might be satisfied with having taken care of two of his three adversaries, and that it was foolhardy to pursue the last man when all he had in the way of a weapon was fifteen inches of tempered steel.

But he kept going, because he was more afraid of failure than he was of death. He had failed his cause in the war, he had failed his family, his homeland, and his fiancée, and he had long ago made up his mind it wasn't worth living if he had to live with another failure.

It was this relentlessness that made him the scourge of outlaws.

Hannibal saw him, and his pistol spat flame and hot lead. Torn thought he heard the shimmy of the bullet, felt the breath of its passage on his cheek. But he didn't flinch, didn't break stride.

The striker savagely reined his mount around. The other horse, still tethered, was in the way, delaying him long enough for Torn to close in. As Hannibal kicked his horse into a leaping start, Torn lunged for the striker, hoping to drag him out of the saddle. Hannibal brought his gun to bear. Torn struck at the mulatto's gun arm with the saber-knife—and missed. Grinning exultantly, Hannibal planted the gun barrel in Torn's chest and pulled the trigger.

CHAPTER 8

DURING THE WAR SOME HAD DECLARED THAT CLAY TORN'S LIFE was charmed. Thirteen horses had been killed out from under him. In the course of the battle of Chancellorsville his uniform had been rent by seven bullets, and yet he had come through that scrape without a mark on him.

Torn had never put much faith in that assertion, but when the hammer of Hannibal's pistol fell on an empty chamber, he became a believer.

He slashed again with the saber-knife, and this time the blade bit deeply into the striker's forearm. The gun slipped from his grasp. Torn grabbed a handful of Hannibal's vest. The horse stretched into a gallop. Torn was jerked off his feet and dragged. Hannibal struck downward with a massive, rock-hard fist, landing a terrible blow on Torn's shoulder. Jolts of incredible pain seared through Torn's body. Again Hannibal struck. Torn couldn't hold on under this battering. He fell, sprawling in the weeds. The striker galloped away.

Trying to ignore the pain, striving to swallow the bitter taste of failure, Torn got to his feet and ran to the second horse. The animal was tethered to a wagon wheel leaning against the back wall of the shanty. Pulling the reins free, he swung into the saddle. The horse responded readily when he kicked it into a gallop.

He still wasn't about to give up trying to get Hannibal.

But when he saw that Torn wasn't through, Hannibal stopped trying to flee. He wheeled his mount sharply, and for the first time Torn recognized for what it was the leather sheath strapped to the striker's back.

Reaching behind him, Hannibal drew a cane knife from the sheath. The wide, single-edged blade, two feet long, glimmered in a silver shred of starlight. With a bloodcurdling yell, the mulatto steered his horse straight at Torn, brandishing the cane knife overhead.

Fighting with blades on horseback was nothing new to Torn. He was confident he could offset Hannibal's superior strength with experience. As they met, Torn deftly parried a vicious overhead stroke. Steel rang against steel in a shower of sparks. As they passed, Torn tried to reach Hannibal with a backhand slash, but the striker anticipated it and struck it aside with the cane knife.

They wheeled their horses and met again. To his chagrin Torn realized the mulatto possessed skill as well as strength. And, all other things being equal, the saber-knife was no match for the longer, heavier cane knife. As they passed the second time it was all Torn could do to keep from being decapitated.

So when they clashed for the third time, Torn resorted to trickery. He deliberately left himself open to a blow to the head, and when Hannibal accepted the invitation and attempted to cleave his skull in two, Torn slipped sideways in the saddle and sliced the latigo of Hannibal's saddle in half.

The striker's hull was an old Spanish single rig, with the girth well forward of the fender and easy to reach with the saber-knife. When Torn cut the latigo, he cut the horse—there was no help for it. The animal snorted and crow-hopped violently. This sent Hannibal and the saddle hurtling through the air.

Turning his horse, Torn headed for the spot where the mulatto had landed. The riderless mount was galloping away. He spotted the saddle in the tall weeds. But there was no trace of Hannibal. Torn cursed the darkness and kept his horse circling, trying to look in every direction at once.

And then the striker came lunging out of the weeds with the agility of a panther. He no longer had the cane knife, but before Torn could bring his own blade into play, Hannibal was on him, knocking him clean out of the saddle.

Torn fell poorly and nearly blacked out. He got unsteadily to his feet and dived sideways as Hannibal, now astride Torn's horse, tried to run him down. The river pirate laughed harshly, checked the horse, and turned to look back.

"You fight good!" he roared. "Someday we fight again." He shook his fist at Torn and galloped away, his crazy laughter ringing in Torn's ears.

Torn experienced a strong and bitter sense of failure as he wearily got to his feet once more. It struck him that of the three men he had tried to apprehend, Hannibal was the most dangerous, and he regretted the mulatto's escape.

He had the feeling, as well, that he was extremely lucky to be alive. Hannibal was a natural-born fighter. Strong, quick, talented—and deadly. Seldom had Torn felt as though he had met his match, but he felt that way now.

And somehow he knew that Hannibal was right.

They would fight again, and the next time one of them wouldn't walk away.

CHAPTER 9

WHEN TORN RETURNED TO THE FRONT OF THE SHANTY, HE SAW Harlan Cratchett wading through the weeds, holding a lantern aloft to light his way. A double-barreled shotgun was under his arm.

"I heard gunfire," he said. "What's going on here, Judge Torn?"

"You were right about Sikes. He's one of Jack Jenkins's bunch."

Cratchett stared at the bodies of Sikes and Blacky, at the collapsed porch of the shack, and finally, in amazement, at a bloodied and disheveled Torn.

"I had a strong gut hunch about that jasper. Is he dead?"

Returning the saber-knife to its shoulder rig, Torn knelt beside Sikes to determine just that. The striker's face was a swollen, bloodied mess, but his pulse was strong.

"No, he's still with us."

"This one sure ain't." Blacky lay at Cratchett's feet, and the old-timer callously prodded the striker's corpse with the toe of his boot. "What happened?"

"Sikes met two men. They—"

"Two men?" Cratchett searched the ground for another body.

"The other one got away."

"What did he look like? Who was he?"

"They called him Hannibal."

Cratchett's jaw dropped. "You're plumb lucky to be alive, Judge."

"I've been thinking the same thing."

"Yep, I've heard of this Hannibal feller, all right. Some folks around here use him to scare their children into doing right. He's the bogeyman. There's talk he poles up and down the river in the dark of night on a raft made from the bones of his victims. 'Course that's all hogwash, but he's a cold-blooded killer, and there ain't no doubt about that. Killin' is what he does best. He likes it. Jenkins uses him to keep the other strikers in line. Y'see, Hannibal is mighty loyal to Jenkins, and the strikers know he'll do whatever Jenkins says to do. It's usually bloody work, but Hannibal don't blink an eye."

Which explained, mused Torn, Hannibal's presence in this meeting between Sikes and Blacky. The mulatto had been here to remind Sikes of the terrible consequences of failure.

Cratchett was anxiously peering into the blackness beyond the reassuring reach of the lantern's mustard-yellow light. The knowledge that Hannibal was anywhere in the vicinity clearly made him nervous.

Torn could see this in Cratchett's expression and posture, and he could fully sympathize. He felt an uncomfortable tingle between his shoulder blades just thinking about Hannibal lurking out there in the night, and he doubted the feeling would go away as long as Hannibal ran free.

A few men were so thoroughly evil and eminently dangerous that they had that effect on others.

Torn had known two others cut from the same cloth. One had been Karl Schmidt, the Yankee sergeant-of-the-guard at Point Lookout Prison, a man utterly vile and vicious—a man Torn had slain, during his daring escape, without hesitation or a twinge of remorse. The other had been a man named Jurgens, a twisted brute who had derived sick pleasure from butchering defenseless women. In both cases Torn had taken another's life without leaving a mark on his conscience.

"You say they were meeting," remarked Cratchett. "What fur?"

Torn told him, succinctly.

"Lord A'mighty, that sounds just like something Jenkins would do," Cratchett declared. "Nobody else would dare even dream up such a scheme."

"Well, I don't think he'll try it now. At least not on the *Sultana.*"

"Reckon you saved a lot of lives, Judge."

Torn made no comment. He borrowed Cratchett's lantern and searched for his Colt. When he found the Peacemaker, he took the precaution of reloading it before sliding it back into the holster.

Giving the lantern back to Cratchett, he picked Sikes up bodily and draped him over a shoulder.

"We ain't got no jail in Hard Times," said Cratchett.

"I'm taking him to St. Louis with me."

"I have a feelin' the *Sultana's* captain won't care for that."

"He won't have much say in the matter. Sikes is a federal prisoner, and I'm going to make sure he's put away for a very long time."

CHAPTER

10

BACK AT THE HOTEL TORN TIED UP SIKES WITH STOUT ROPE provided by Cratchett. He gagged the striker and left him on the floor in the dining room. Then he sat down at the table, tired and sore, and gratefully accepted Cratchett's offer of some moonshine. The old-timer was generous, and the 'shine smoothed out the nerves and killed some of the pain.

Cratchett took a close look at Torn's hands. There was a lot of blood. Most of it was Sikes's blood, but Torn's knuckles—already much scarred, noted the old-timer—were nicked and scraped and swollen.

"You pounded on him pretty hard," Cratchett commented.

"He has a hard head."

Cratchett gazed a moment at the unconscious striker laid out on the floor. "If you got some notion of trying to get him to turn on Jenkins, you better forget it. Be a waste of time. Like I said before, a striker knows he's as good as dead if he gets a case of loose lips. I'll get some salve for those hands of yours, and something for bandages."

Torn was rinsing the blood off his hands in a bucket of water when Rebecca Ashbrook appeared. She was dressed as she had been earlier, but she'd let her hair down. White-gold ringlets caressed her shoulders.

"Ma'am, you ought not to be here," said Cratchett. "What would your father say?"

She stared at Sikes, then Torn. "I heard shots. My father is asleep." She was quite composed. "Mr. Torn, you're hurt."

"It's nothing, ma'am."

She stepped in and took over, just the same, drying his hands with a clean cloth and applying a salve to his wounds.

"I can manage," said Torn. He had spent so many years taking care of himself that it was embarrassing to have a woman fuss over him.

"Just hush."

He had to smile. "I thought the sight of blood ruined your appetite, Miss Ashbrook."

She was bending over, gently laying on the salve, and her face was very close to his, and a faint fragrance—he thought it was jasmine—came to him, mustering up thoughts of home, the shattered past, another life, another woman.

"It is supposed to, isn't it? I mean, proper young ladies are simply expected to faint at the sight, aren't they? But I've become accustomed to caring for the ill and the injured, Mr. Torn. When we were in Mexico, there was an outbreak of yellow fever. My mother died—I believe my father told you, didn't he? There were a great many sick people, and virtually no qualified physicians. I did what I could to ease their suffering. But there wasn't much I really could do, except to make them as comfortable as possible as they died."

She looked up into his eyes, and he saw the sadness and the pain these memories cost her.

"You must be very brave," he said.

"It had nothing to do with courage. Or cowardice. Nothing, even, to do with right or wrong. Sometimes we are forced to do what must be done, whether we like it or not. Whether it is right or wrong."

Torn got the impression she was discussing something beyond her actions in Mexico during an epidemic years ago. The remarks puzzled him, but he didn't ask her to explain. He could tell she didn't intend to elaborate on the subject, whatever it was, and so he was left hanging.

She wrapped his hands with strips of clean linen, tearing the last six inches of each piece down the middle, taking the two halves around the hand in opposite directions, and tying them in a knot to hold the dressing firmly in place. He noted, too, how soft and delicate her hands were, compared with his big, strong, scarred paws, and how cool and gentle her touch.

When she was done, he flexed his gun hand to make sure the dressing did not interfere and practiced drawing his Peacemaker.

"Will there be more trouble?" Rebecca asked calmly.

"No. I don't think so."

Again she looked at the unconscious striker. "Is he an outlaw?"

"I knew it when I first laid eyes on the scoundrel," declared Cratchett. "He's one of Jack Jenkins's men.

They were planning to board the *Sultana* and rob everybody aboard. Then they were going to kill—"

"Cratchett!"

"Sorry, Judge, I—"

"Judge?" Rebecca turned to Torn, her eyes wide.

Torn grimaced. Cratchett was mortified.

"Every time I open my big mouth, seems like I stick
my foot in it," he lamented.

"So you're a judge," said Rebecca, with a wry smile.

The cat was out of the bag, and Torn knew it was
pointless to practice further deception. If John Ashbrook *was* a swindler, he would certainly steer clear of
Torn now.

"Yes, ma'am. Federal judge."

"I venture to say my father believed you were something else entirely."

"I don't own anything but the clothes on my back. I
lost everything in the war. Home, family, everything."
As it seemed to be the time for complete candor, he
added, "I also lost the woman I love."

She put a hand, light as a feather, on his arm. "I am
terribly, terribly sorry."

"You don't need to worry, Miss Ashbrook," Torn said
gruffly, quick to change the subject to one a lot less
painful. "The *Sultana* and everyone on her will be safe."

"I know you mean that, and I thank you." She headed
for the door, pausing on the threshold to look back,
smiling pensively. "But life is full of surprises, isn't it?
And most of them are unpleasant."

After she had gone, Cratchett poured Torn another
dose of moonshine. The old-timer was crestfallen.

"If you want to kick me into next week, Judge, I won't
hold it against you."

"Forget it. The truth is always the best road to travel."

"You look plumb worn to a frazzle. I'll watch Sikes, if you want to get some sleep. You know, an old man like me don't need much shut-eye. 'Course I wouldn't blame you if you didn't trust me."

Torn knew he could. Cratchett was begging for an opportunity to redeem himself after betraying Torn's confidence.

So he agreed to the arrangement, much to Cratchett's surprise. Trudging up to his room, he stretched out fully clothed on the bed and, this time, fell asleep immediately, the Colt under his pillow.

CHAPTER

11

EARLY THE NEXT MORNING CRATCHETT TOOK THEM TO THE landing to meet the *Sultana* on its upriver haul from New Orleans. He used an old Dougherty ambulance cart for the purpose. The Dougherty was a four-wheeled spring wagon with a permanent canvas top and three transverse benches. Canvas sides, still bearing the green Maltese cross, were rolled up and tied, due to the already oppressive heat. The luggage was secured in the rear boot, a chain-supported platform covered with more canvas. The old ambulance was pulled by two mules.

Torn sensed no animosity or fear on Ashbrook's part, and as he had to assume that Rebecca had informed her father that he was a federal judge, he began to wonder if he had done the man a grave injustice by suspecting him, without any real evidence, of being a swindler. Ashbrook did know about Sikes and the Jenkins plan, as evidenced by his remarks as they were boarding the Dougherty in front of the hotel.

"Thank God you had the courage to apprehend this rascal, Clay. I shudder to think what might have happened had this bloodthirsty scheme gone undiscovered."

"We might have had an unpleasant trip," agreed Torn. He fired a curious glance at Rebecca, but she scrupulously avoided his gaze. What Ashbrook knew of the facts remained a mystery, as Cratchett was in a hurry to get them loaded up and to the river.

Ashbrook and his daughter rode on the forward bench, directly behind the driver's seat. Sikes, his hands tied behind his back, shared the middle bench with Torn. The striker's bruised and swollen face had a belligerent cast. He hadn't uttered a word since regaining consciousness.

As Cratchett whipped up the mules and the Dougherty rattled down the street of the sleepy town, Torn spotted two buzzards circling lazily in the brightening sky, in the vicinity of the abandoned shack where the corpse of the striker named Blacky still lay. Cratchett had promised to give the dead man a decent burial. Torn had seen thousands of dead left to rot on battlefields during the war, and he firmly believed that every man, no matter how despicable in life, deserved better than that in death. He hoped Cratchett would deliver on his promise before the buzzards—called by some wit the sacred bird of the South—got too far in their grisly work.

They left Hard Times before sunrise, when the coming day was little more than a ribbon of pearly light in the eastern sky. The road took them over the levee, across a half mile of weed-overgrown bottomland—where the Mississippi had once flowed—and finally through a stretch of wooded hills.

The landing proved to be a wharf supported by stout pilings, at the foot of a grassy knoll around which the road curled to reach the river. By this time the sun had climbed above the line of trees on the far shore, more than a half mile away, lending a sheen of bronze to the placid surface of the mighty river, broken here by the black shape of a floating log, there by an arrowhead ripple, and almost everywhere by the circle sign of feeding fish.

Torn had seen the Mississippi on many occasions, but it never failed to impress him with its sheer majesty. By comparison it put to shame every so-called river he had crossed in his travels on the frontier. He felt humbled by its raw, slumbering power.

To the north of the landing, a towhead—a newly formed island—split the river in two. To the south it curled out of sight around a stern, red-flanked bluff. There was no sign of the boat they had come to meet. Cratchett reminded them that river-passage schedules were imprecise. The Mississippi was always full of mischief, declared the old-timer. She was forever putting up new hazards and obstacles, and dispensing with the old ones as soon as rivermen had overcome them, which made every passage a new and often dangerous experience. There were very few steamboats, mentioned Cratchett, that died a "natural death." This comment amused Torn, but it etched apprehension on Ashbrook's dignified features, and Cratchett apologized for being so insensitive, explaining that he suffered from a chronic foot-in-mouth ailment.

They settled down to wait, and Cratchett lingered. He seemed reluctant to part company. He talked tirelessly, for the most part about the river he loved and feared. For the first time since meeting Cratchett Torn recognized that the old-timer was a lonely man. His wife had run off, his town was dying. Not too many people passed through Hard Times anymore, and Cratchett was putting off saying his good-byes to three who had.

As the morning aged, the heat grew worse. Rebecca sat on a small trunk on the shady side of the Dougherty. Ashbrook kept mopping his florid face with a sopping-wet handkerchief. Torn stayed on the wharf, and kept Sikes with him, as far away as possible from Miss Ashbrook.

A couple of hours passed before the striker spoke. "Where you taking me?"

"St. Louis."

"What for?"

"To stand trial."

"I ain't done nothing."

"You were planning to."

"You can't put me in jail for that."

"Watch me."

"You'll never get me anywhere near St. Louis." Sikes sneered.

"You figure Jenkins will try to rescue you?"

Sikes was silent for a moment, gazing across the river. When he replied, all the belligerence was gone, replaced by quiet despair. "I figure he'll kill me. I'm a dead man."

"I'll make you a deal," said Torn. "You testify that Jenkins planned the taking of the *Sultana,* and I'll guarantee your safety."

Sikes barked a bitter laugh. "You will, huh? You sure do think high of yourself, mister. Jack Jenkins'll make short work of you."

"What about it?"

"Go to hell. I took an oath."

It was Torn's turn to laugh. "Honor among thieves."

"I'm dead, one way or the other. So why should I do you any favors?"

Torn shrugged and let it go at that.

A little while later a couple of youngsters showed up to fish off the wharf while they awaited the arrival of the packet. One had a fishing pole. The other tied his line to his big toe and let his foot dangle over the water. An old yellow dog accompanied them. The dog checked out all the strangers and took a strong dislike to Sikes. It lowered its head and tail and bared its fangs and made menacing noises deep in its throat. Sikes cursed a blue streak and tried to land a kick. The dog latched onto his pants leg. Sikes started hollering at the top of his lungs. Torn ran the dog off, thinking all along that animals were very good judges of character.

A few minutes later one of the youngsters cried out, "Steamboat a-comin'!"

Peering downriver, Torn saw the side-wheeler *Sultana* gracefully glide into view around the bend.

CHAPTER

12

The *Sultana* was a handsome sight, a floating palace, and in the opinion of all one of the grandest vessels to ever ply the waters of the Mississippi.

She was three hundred feet long, drew only five feet of water, and at the moment was capable of plowing resolutely against the strong current of the deceptively placid river at a speed averaging ten miles an hour. Once around the bend, she "straightened down" into the "reach"; a few minutes later a bell rang three times, the captain's order to land.

The steamboat veered gradually closer to the east bank, out of the main channel. She churned past the wharf, a stone's throw away, before the engines were silenced at the ring of the captain's bell. As the mighty side-wheels were stilled steam shrilled through the gauge cocks. The current carried the boat backward and sideways. Roustabouts on the boiler deck wielded long poles to cushion the impact with the wharf. A deckhand stood balanced on the end of the broad stage run out over the port bow, a coil of heavy rope in hand. When the *Sultana* neared the wharf, he made a bold and agile leap ashore and made the side-wheeler fast, lashing the cordelle to a sturdy mooring post.

While the landing was executed Torn had plenty of time to get a good look at the side-wheeler, stem to stern. Her twin smokestacks, forward of the pilothouse, were crowned and banded with white iron collars. Columns of wood smoke, blackened with pitch—a custom on the river when a steamboat made a landing—billowed from the towering stacks. Suspended between the stacks on white wrought-iron was a gilded device bearing the golden-star-and-scimitar insignia of the *Sultana* on a scarlet background. High on the stacks were the passing lights, red and green storm lanterns, used in night running.

The main deck resembled a huge open warehouse, but for the housing, forward, of the boilers and engines. The *Sultana* boasted eight boilers, which consumed on the average a cord of wood per hour. The main deck was cluttered with stacks of cordwood, sacks, crates, barrels, two wagons, and what Torn estimated to be at least fifty "deck passengers" with their belongings and, in some cases, livestock.

Above the main deck was the boiler deck. Here were the staterooms, the saloon, and the dining room reserved for first-class passengers. The staterooms were so called because they bore the names of the states in the Union rather than numbers, a tradition in the riverboat trade. They lined both sides of the dining room and opened onto a narrow promenade.

The roof of the boiler deck was called the hurricane

deck, where the "texas"—the cabins for the captain and mates, and quarters for the deck hands—was located. Atop the texas was the pilothouse.

The paddle boxes were painted white and red, and bore the vessel's name as well as the star-and-scimitar insignia. The boiler, hurricane, and texas decks were ornamented with white guardrails and plenty of ginger-bread. Though he had never been aboard the *Sultana,* Torn had taken passage on comparable packets, and he knew the vessel would be decked out with all the trap-pings of a luxury hotel.

The main deck was crowded—"deck passage" was the cheapest rate on the river—but there were very few people watching the landing from the promenades of the upper decks. First-class passage cost about twenty-five dollars; Torn was of a mind to travel that way, and it appeared he would have no trouble obtaining a state-room.

It wasn't that he objected to mingling with the poor folks or sleeping on the deck. He had been brought up in luxury, as close to royalty as one could get in this country, but that life was a distant memory. Since those days of elegant comfort he had endured the privations of two years of war and sixteen months of hell in Point Lookout Prison, where having a ragged blanket to sleep on had been a luxury, and in ten years on the frontier had spent most of the time sleeping on hard ground beneath the stars. But he had the money to partake of the best the *Sultana* had to offer, thanks to Cratchett's more than fair offer for the chestnut he had dragged into Hard Times the day before, and he thought it would be wise to keep Sikes out of circulation as much as pos-sible.

It didn't come as a surprise to him that the *Sultana* lacked first-class passengers. The halcyon days of the riverboat were long gone. The railroads were faster and cheaper and more convenient for the majority of travelers. The iron road could take a person where he wanted, when he wanted. The last ten years had witnessed a tremendous rail expansion. Just as the steamboat had killed keelboating by reducing river-passage time, the railroad was using the same rope to strangle the steamboat trade.

Once his business in Bayou Sorrel had been concluded, Torn could have ridden to Baton Rouge and caught a train to St. Louis, but he had wanted to ride the river, conscious of the fact that the day would soon be at hand when the opportunity no longer presented itself. He was glad of the decision. Had he gone to Baton Rouge instead of Hard Times, the side-wheeler now before him in all its gaily painted glory, and all her passengers, might have ended up at the bottom of the Mississippi.

The stage was run out onto the wharf. It was really just an oversized gangplank, large enough to accommodate a full-size wagon, and was commonly called a stage because, in the old days, minstrel shows and similar entertainments had been held on it for the benefit of the locals.

Only one passenger disembarked: a lanky youngster who appeared to be fresh off the farm. He carried his belongings in a burlap sack slung over his shoulder. This seemed to Torn a demonstration of the decline of the riverboat: the *Sultana* had made a landing here to discharge one customer and take on four more. That wouldn't have happened in the heyday of the steamboat, before the war. But nowadays the packets were trying to scrape by, and every fare counted.

When the young man reached the wharf, Cratchett was there to greet him. The old-timer offered him a ride into Hard Times, and the newcomer nodded and headed for the Dougherty. Cratchett came over to Torn.

"Go west, young man," said Torn, echoing the famous words of newspaperman Horace Greeley.

Cratchett nodded. "By the looks of him I'd say he ain't never been this far off the old homestead before. Can't say as I blame him. I see a lot of younkers pass through, heading for the frontier, and fame and fortune."

"I hope he finds it. Most don't."

"Well, I'll take him as far as Hard Times and give him a free meal. It'll be a long hard road for the younker, so that's the least I can do."

Torn glanced across the wharf at the young man, now hunkered down in the shade of the old ambulance wagon, and he wondered how the boy would fare on the frontier. Big dreams and good intentions were no match for bad luck, and there was plenty of bad luck waiting for those who were westward bound. Sometimes men took the wrong turn and found themselves walking on the wrong side of the law.

Torn hoped the young man would be able to stick to the straight and narrow. Most of the outlaws he had dealt with had started out as ordinary men who got down on their luck and resorted to desperate deeds.

These thoughts brought Jack Jenkins to mind. Jenkins was one who did not fit this mold. He was no ordinary man. By all accounts he was a criminal mastermind, brilliant, amoral, and unhindered by conscience.

It concerned Torn that Jenkins had been able to operate with impunity for so long. Something had to be done. The *Sultana* was probably safe, but what of other riverboats? In all likelihood Jenkins would try his audacious, bloodthirsty scheme on some other packet. Torn didn't know how he was going to do it, but he knew he had to find a way to stop Jenkins once and for all.

Cratchett's thoughts were also on Jenkins. "Hope you can put a stop to the ol' Corpse Maker, Judge," said the old-timer. "I got a feeling that if any one man could do the job, it's you."

Torn shook his head, recalling with admiration the way Cratchett had ventured out with shotgun under arm the night before, drawn by the sound of gunfire. "It's men like you that make the difference," he said. "Honest folk." He gestured at Sikes. "Men like this will always lose, in the long run, as long as there are people like you."

They shook hands and said their so-longs. Cratchett watched Torn head up the stage with Sikes, then turned to the Dougherty where the young man bent on westering awaited.

CHAPTER 13

THE ASHBROOKS HAD PRECEDED TORN ABOARD THE *SULTANA*. The side-wheeler's captain was there to greet them. He was a gaunt, graying, one-armed man in a blue claw-hammer coat complete with gold-braided shoulder bars and yellow-brown nankeen trousers. A couple of porters were dispatched to the wharf to bring the Ashbrook baggage aboard.

When her father introduced her to the captain, Rebecca curtsied, and Torn could tell the steamboat skipper was charmed by her grace and beauty. He experienced a stab of jealousy, and laughed at himself. What made him imagine he had any kind of claim on Rebecca Ashbrook? He could scarcely blame the captain for being smitten. Most red-blooded males would be.

As a steward escorted the Ashbrooks to the boiler deck, Torn reached the top of the stage, Sikes in one hand, his valise—with scabbarded Winchester strapped to it—in the other. The captain's frosty blue eyes flicked from the wrist-bound striker's battered face to the rifle and then fastened with thin and chilly courtesy on Torn.

"Captain Ezra Blake at your service, sir. Mr. Ashbrook informs me there has been an incident in Hard Times. He did not elaborate. I have a feeling that you can."

Torn introduced himself. "This man is my prisoner, Captain. He is one of Jack Jenkins's men."

"I cannot refuse to give you and your prisoner passage, Judge. If I tried, you would have the right to insist. But I hope you realize you are jeopardizing my crew and the other passengers."

"This ship was already in jeopardy," said Torn, irritated by this cool reception. He told Blake of the plot to hold up the *Sultana*.

"You expect from me a debt of gratitude, no doubt," said Blake stiffly. "Perhaps I owe you one. Forgive me if I fail to give it. But you see, sir, I've heard of you. I know you fought for the Rebellion. I am happy to say I fought for the preservation of the Union. My brother gave his life for this great nation. I gave my arm. In my opinion all secessionists are traitors."

"The war is over," said Torn. He gestured at Sikes. "These men are the enemy now."

"Judge Torn, you and I will always be enemies. Mr. Harker!"

A husky, sandy-haired man hurried over.

"Mr. Harker is my first mate," said Blake. "Let your needs be known to him, and he will see to them."

With that, Captain Blake turned sharply on his heel and walked away.

* * *

The mate, Harker, led Torn to the "Kentucky" stateroom, on the starboard side of the boiler deck. The *Sultana*'s twenty-two staterooms were located in the aft portion of the boat, around the dining room, which in turn was behind the main saloon. This was by design, to place the staterooms as far as possible from the engines and boilers. Riverboat machinery was chronically unreliable and had a tendency to blow up. Many were the steamboats that had "died" in that manner. Passengers housed aft had a better chance of survival in that event.

The stateroom was as opulent as Torn had expected. Damask and rich dark wood wainscoting on the walls, red velvet upholstery on the Empire chairs and swansdown divan, a high polish on the teak floor, brass cabin lamps and a couple of gilt-framed oils, and a roomy fourposter that promised the best sleep Torn had had since leaving Ravenoak plantation on the disastrous road to war.

"What do you want to do with *him,* Judge?" asked Harker, looking askance at the sullen Sikes.

"I'd best keep him with me."

Harker nodded and turned to leave. He paused just beyond the doorway, checked the promenade in both directions, and leaned back inside. "For what it's worth, Judge, I overheard what you told the captain, and I want you to know we don't all feel the way he does."

"Thanks," said Torn, surprised.

Harker touched knuckles to forehead in a respectful salute and closed the louvered door on his way out.

"You gonna untie me?" growled Sikes.

"When we get to St. Louis."

"You bastard. I'm gonna kill you first chance I get."

Torn gave him a shove. Sikes sat down hard in a chair.

"You had your chance," said Torn. "If you get to be too much trouble for me, I'll just toss you over the side and be done with you."

"You would too." Sikes sneered, and fear lurked behind his defiance. "You ain't all that different from Jack Jenkins."

"Maybe not much," allowed Torn. "But enough."

A few minutes later Harker returned. "Duke Doniphan would like to see you, Judge, if you got the time."

"I don't know a Duke Doniphan."

"He's one of the pilots. He saw you come aboard." Harker nodded at Sikes. "He says he knows this man."

Torn peered at the striker. Sikes had turned pale.

"He's lying!" exclaimed Sikes. "I don't know no Doniphan."

"Where is he?" Torn asked Harker.

"Pilothouse. I'll watch this yegg, if you want."

Torn's instinct was to trust the *Sultana*'s first mate. He agreed to leave his prisoner in Harker's care.

The pilothouse stood in lofty isolation atop the texas. As Torn reached it the side-wheeler was leaving the wharf. The pilot on duty—the man Torn assumed was Duke Doniphan—was a short wiry individual with leathery, sun-dark skin, a stubborn jaw, and muddy brown eyes that resembled drops of Mississippi river water.

He stood at the wheel with his "cub," a greenhorn kid the likes of which were found on every riverboat. The cub received no wage—he worked in exchange for the opportunity to learn the pilot trade. Though the riverboat industry was in decline, there were still plenty of youths drawn by the romance of being a "knight of the tiller."

Duke's cub was a slight, towheaded youngster with a freckled face. Torn calculated he couldn't possibly be more than fifteen years of age. For all that, he stood half a head taller than the pilot.

The pilothouse sported windows on all sides, and from this vantage point sixty feet above the river, Torn had a magnificent view in every direction. The wheel attended by the pilot and his protégé was ten feet in diameter, a handsome piece of brass-fitted mahogany. The bottom half extended through a hole in the deck to the texas below. Within easy reach of a man at the wheel were several bell ropes attached to large brass bells on the roof of the pilothouse. There was also a speaking tube by which the pilot could communicate with the engine room two decks below.

Doniphan looked around as Torn entered. "You the judge?"

"Yes. Are you Doniphan?"

"That I am. I want to have a word with you about Sikes. Here, boy. Take the wheel."

Doniphan crossed the pilothouse, leaving the cub to wrestle with the massive wheel and alone guide the side-wheeler into the main channel.

"You know Sikes?" asked Torn.

"That I do." Doniphan spoke in a brusque, clipped manner. In spite of his diminutive frame he gave the impression of a man who would take no guff from anyone. Dynamite came in small packages. "Sikes used to be a pilot. He also drank too much. Killed a boat. And a goodly number of passengers and crew, as well. Happened a mile above Island Fourteen. They were going to put him on trial in Memphis, but he broke out of jail."

"And joined up with Jack Jenkins."

"Where in tarnation are you going?" bellowed Doniphan, so loudly and unexpectedly that Torn jumped. It was the cub who received this verbal lightning bolt. "Pull her down, goldurnit! Pull her down! And you want to be a pilot! Lord help us." Doniphan snorted derisively, turned back to Torn, and quite calmly remarked, "Yes, Harker overheard your conversation with Captain Blake."

"You don't seem surprised."

"Nothing Jenkins could do would surprise me. Hear you fought for the Confederacy. So did I. Louisiana Tigers. Don't mind Blake. That missing arm still plagues him something fierce. I'm his enemy, too, but he can't do nothing to me. The line hired me, and federal law protects me from crazy captains. I don't have to take orders that would jeopardize the boat. I—*snatch her, goldurnit! Where are you going to now, boy? Are you stone blind? Don't you see that snag, for Chrissakes?"*

Torn was astonished. Doniphan had not been paying the river any attention at all—or so it seemed. And yet, sure enough, the snag was there. Red-faced and tight-lipped, the cub turned the wheel sharply.

"So you might have saved the *Sultana,* Judge," said Doniphan. "But then again you might have signed her death warrant."

"I don't follow."

"You're the law, right?"

"That's right."

"Then you must know that the problem all along has been that Jenkins gets others to do his dirty deeds for him, and if they get caught, they're too gol-durn afraid of Jenkins to talk, so he's never implicated. Have I got it right, so far?"

"Right."

"But Sikes is facing a rope, Judge. His drunken negligence three years ago cost forty people their lives. And if I know Sikes, he'll sing like a canary to stay alive."

"He doesn't seem inclined to talk."

Doniphan smirked. "Hope springs eternal. He's just bluffing. Wait until he's standing on that trapdoor with a noose around his worthless neck."

"You seem to know a lot about him."

"That I do," repeated Doniphan, through clenched teeth. "It makes sense, Jenkins wanting him aboard to take over this here wheel when the time came. But I bet Jenkins nor Sikes, neither one, counted on me being one of the *Sultana*'s pilots. You see—*you going to hold her down all gol-durn day, you nitwit? Let her go! Meet her! Meet her, for Chrissakes!* Because you see, Judge, I was the other pilot for the *Tuscarora*. That's the boat Sikes killed. I durn near drowned, myself. And for a long while thereafter I had the devil's own time getting work. Guilt by association, ain't that what they call it? Yeah, I know Sikes, all right."

"You said I may have signed the *Sultana*'s death warrant."

Doniphan nodded curtly. He was an extremely blunt, straightforward man who spoke his mind and didn't care who liked what he had to say. "Because Jenkins took a risk with Sikes. He's bound to know Sikes is unreliable. Now he's obliged to shut Sikes up, permanently. So I figure he'll go on ahead and try to take this boat. He'll do what he planned and silence Sikes into the bargain. I could be wrong. But I doubt it."

CHAPTER 14

HARLAN CRATCHETT WAS IN A GOOD MOOD ALL DAY, NOTWITH-standing the fact that he had to perform an unpleasant task in regard to the remains of the striker named Blacky.

For one thing having the youngster to talk to was a stroke of luck. The departure of Torn and the Ashbrooks had depressed him. For Cratchett personally, the worst part of the demise of Hard Times was that there just weren't very many interesting people to talk to. There were still a few people left in town, but none had the wherewithal to engage the old-timer in the lively conversations he enjoyed so much.

The second reason for his good humor was the knowledge that Judge Torn had thwarted the most diabolical, blackhearted scheme he had ever heard of, right here in his own backyard, so to speak. Now that was something to talk about for years to come!

He started with the young man fresh off the *Sultana,*

who said his name was Grady. Cratchett told of last night's incident in all its gory detail.

Grady was all ears. He listened with breathless excitement as the old-timer recounted, and embellished, the desperate life-and-death struggle between Judge Torn and three of the vilest rogues in the land. It set Grady's pulse to racing better than any dime novel could. It was just this kind of adventure that had compelled him to run away from a lifetime of drudgery on the family homestead.

"That tall feller dressed all in black," said Grady, "the one at the landing—he was the judge?"

Cratchett nodded. "And he's the only argument I need to prove to you that you'd best not take up no lawless ways, boy, or have any truck with desperadoes. 'Cause iffen you make that mistake, you'll have to answer to Judge Torn, or a man just like him. Hard men with cold eyes and quick guns and no mercy for wrongdoers. That's the way the law's got to be out on the frontier. Swift and terrible. Old Testament. Eye for an eye."

To further make his point Cratchett enlisted the young man to help him bury Blacky—this in exchange for a free meal and a free night's lodging, if the boy wanted it. Grady eagerly agreed to help. But his enthusiasm waned when they came upon Blacky's corpse.

It was early afternoon by then, the hottest part of one of the hottest days of the year, and the sweltering heat had had a grisly effect on the striker's mortal remains. The corpse was bloated. Flies swarmed all over it. The stench of decay washed every trace of color from Grady's face. And when the corpse moved, as gas escaped, the callow youngster uttered a strangled yelp, whirled around, and retched violently.

"This here's what comes of wrongdoing," declared Cratchett, with a righteous air.

He said no more on the subject, figuring he had made his point on Grady. Frontier boot hills were full of good men gone bad, and the old-timer hoped that Grady would remember the lesson he had learned today and escape that sorry fate.

They planted Blacky, returned to the hotel, and whiled away the afternoon. Cratchett regaled the young wanderer with tales of his own youthful adventures. Grady was shaken by his ordeal, but, come suppertime, had recovered sufficiently to dispatch plenty of grub.

After dinner they talked some more. Grady was a little homesick, and intimidated by the great unknown he was about to venture into, so the old-timer kept him company as long as he could keep his eyes open. It was very late when Cratchett turned in.

His quarters were downstairs, just off the dining room. He gave Grady a choice of the upstairs rooms. He tried to read some from his Bible, but his eyelids felt heavy as anvils, and in short order he was sound asleep.

In the eerie stillness of the early-morning hours he was jolted awake by a sound from beyond his door. His first thought was that the sound—whatever it had been —had been made by Grady, so when he went to investigate, he left his shotgun leaning against the wall beside his bed.

When he opened the door, rough hands grabbed him, hustled him across the room, and slammed him into a chair at the long table. A gun barrel was pressed against his temple.

He did not dare move even to look up at the man standing beside him and threatening him with the pistol. Instead he stared at a second man, this one seated at the other end of the table. A lantern had been lighted and placed on the floor behind the second man's chair, and this backlight obscured his features. In spite of this Cratchett sensed the man's great physical power and an aura of cold, menacing cruelty.

"Good morning, Mr. Cratchett. Sorry to wake you."

The man's tone was low and cordial, his voice resonant and not unpleasant, the words articulated in an educated way.

"What's . . . what's going on?" managed the old-timer.

A soft chuckle. "All in good time, my friend."

From the direction of the staircase came the sound of a scuffle, a cry of pain. A moment later Grady appeared in the doorway, white as a sheet, in the grasp of a man Cratchett did recognize.

"Hannibal!"

The burly mulatto grinned, then tightened his stranglehold on Grady as the youngster tried to break away. Grady stopped struggling and gasped for air, on the verge of passing out.

"Let him go!" yelled Cratchett, more concerned about Grady than the gun at his own head. "You're killing him, you sorry bastard."

"Not yet, Hannibal," said the man at the other end of the table. "Don't kill him yet."

The mulatto relented, but he kept Grady under restraint.

"He's just an innocent kid," said Cratchett. "Let him go."

Again the soft chuckle. "Do you know who I am?"

Cratchett shook his head. He had a hunch, and hoped and prayed he was wrong.

The man said, "My name is Jack Jenkins."

Somehow Cratchett knew he was going to die.

CHAPTER

15

Now that he knew he was going to die, an iron calm overcame Harlan Cratchett. The fear subsided, replaced by cold indignation.

"You're not welcome under my roof, Jenkins. Get the hell out. I won't have scum like the three of you—"

The man next to Cratchett rapped him viciously across the skull with the barrel of his gun. The old-timer slumped sideways out of his chair, moaning, and sprawled on the floor. The excruciating pain made him feel like vomiting, and he had to fight to avoid blacking out.

With a crooked grin the man knocked the chair out of his way and bent over the suffering Cratchett with gun raised. He wasn't through pistol-whipping the defenseless old man.

"Finch."

Jenkins didn't raise his voice, but Cratchett's assailant froze.

"That's enough," said Jenkins.

"Did you hear what he called us?"

"A man is entitled to his opinion. Help him up."

Disgruntled, Finch righted the chair, hauled Cratchett to his feet, and planted him in the chair, none too gently. Cratchett sagged, caught himself by gripping the edge of the table in front of him. He blinked at the crazy dancing lights in his eyes and felt the warm trickle of blood on his temple.

"Mr. Cratchett," said Jenkins, "I know about you. I know about almost everyone on the river, from Island Number Ten to Bonnet Carré. For instance, I know you have been quite outspoken in your opposition against me."

Cratchett barked a harsh laugh. "Every honest man stands against you, Jenkins. What do you think you are, anyway? You're a murderer and a thief—and you expect to have public opinion on your side?"

"Every honest man? We could debate whether there really is such a creature. I've left you alone because you're a harmless old fool. But now I have a bone to pick with you. You have interfered with my plans. I can't let that go unpunished."

"Let the boy alone. He doesn't have nothing to do with this. He's just passing through. Got off the boat today and heads west tomorrow."

"I ain't done nothing against you, Mr. Jenkins, sir," whined Grady, his voice quavering. "Don't hurt me."

"I have no quarrel with you, son," replied Jenkins, his tone almost paternal. "Was it the *Sultana* you came up on?"

Grady nodded, his Adam's apple bobbing as he tried to swallow the lump of abject fear in his throat.

"Up from New Orleans."

"N-no sir. Plaquemine."

"Don't tell him nothing, boy," said Cratchett.

Finch nudged the old man with his pistol. "Shut the hell up."

"Are there many passengers aboard the *Sultana,* young man?" Jenkins asked Grady.

Grady's head turned rapidly this way and that as he looked from Jenkins at one end of the table to Cratchett at the other, back and forth, trying to decide what to do. He knew that Cratchett was a good man, and no one had to tell him that Jenkins was evil, and he knew what was right, but if he did what was right, he could die. When it came to deciding whether to live or die, right and wrong didn't matter much.

"Answer," hissed Hannibal, whispering in Grady's ear. "Answer or I snap your scrawny neck."

"I . . . I reckon so," babbled Grady. "Lots of folks on the deck where I was. A couple of families with wagons and livestock and such headed for St. Louis. They said they were gonna join a wagon train. I thought about going with them. Then I . . . I decided to get off here and go to Texas." Grady looked about ready to weep as he considered how bad that decision had proved to be. "And . . . and there were others. Some going up to Memphis, or Natchez, or—"

"What about on the deck above?" interrupted Jenkins.

"I don't know. I didn't—"

Jenkins pounded the table with his fist. "Don't lie to me, son. You're young, and the young are by nature curious. Don't tell me you didn't go up there."

"No, sir. I mean, yes, sir, I did. Just to have a look around. One of the crewmen told me most of the cabins up there was empty. I just saw a few men, all dressed up to the nines, in that big room—"

"The main saloon," said Jenkins. "Yes. Who boarded the *Sultana* today?"

"There was this older gentlemen, and a young lady with him. I figured he was her father. And . . . and there was a man in black. And he had a man with him, tied up, looked half beat to death."

"Describe this last man."

"He was a big man. Red hair." Grady shook his head.

"So Sikes is alive," said Jenkins. "And on the *Sultana*. I thought so. You buried one man, Mr. Cratchett. We dug him up. It was Blacky. Blacky was a good man. One of my best lieutenants. And so I wondered about Sikes. Now I know. Who is this man in black, Mr. Cratchett?"

"I'm not telling you anything."

"I see. What's your name, son?"

"Grady, sir."

"Sit down, Grady."

Shaking like a leaf, Grady sat down at the table.

Jenkins said, "Finch, if the boy moves, shoot him."

"My pleasure." Finch grinned and moved around behind Grady's chair.

Jenkins leaned forward, arms on the table. Cratchett noticed a heavy gold ring on the man's right little finger. A black stone was set into the ring. The old-timer stared at the ring and refused to look around as Hannibal circled around behind him. He began to mumble the Lord's Prayer.

"Mr. Cratchett," said Jenkins, his voice deadly and silken. "Who was that man in black?"

". . . Thy Kingdom come, Thy will be done . . ."

Jenkins chuckled. "You've had a good life, old man."

". . . As we forgive those who trespass against us . . ."

Jenkins nodded.

Hannibal drew the cane knife out of the long leather sheath strapped to his back. The blade, poised high overhead for an instant, glimmered like molten gold in the lamplight. Then the mulatto brought it sweeping down.

Grady howled in terror, a hoarse, guttural wail, as Hannibal beheaded Harlan Cratchett.

16

CRATCHETT'S HEAD STRUCK THE TABLE ONCE AND ROLLED OFF onto the floor. His twitching torso spilled sideways out of the chair. Blood spewed from the severed neck. Grady felt the warm spray of blood on his face. The lantern on the floor behind Jenkins's chair cast the outlaw leader's shadow over the entire room, leaving it in semidarkness. Grady could not see clearly, but he could see enough of the horror that his skin crawled and his hair stood on end. Howling like a madman, he looked down at the splatter of blood on his clothes, at the glistening black splash of it on the table. Then his eyes rolled up in their sockets and he fainted, sliding to the floor.

Jenkins sat unmoving at the end of the table.

"Want me to kill the boy?" asked Hannibal hopefully, a mad brightness in his black eyes.

"No."

Hannibal was disappointed. He wiped the blade of his

cane knife on Cratchett's shirt and returned it to its sheath.

Finch watched the mulatto with ill-disguised loathing. "Christ," he muttered. "Could have just shot him."

"Too noisy," said Jenkins offhandedly. "Besides, I want to leave a message. I want people to remember what happens to someone who crosses me."

"What are you going to do? Leave a note with your name on it?"

Jenkins was sternly silent for a moment. Finch was teetering on the brink of insubordination; Cratchett's execution had shaken him, putting his nerves on edge. Jenkins's icy silence warned him that he was on the verge of going too far.

Finch was a desperado of the first order. A bank robber and murderer who only recently had joined Jenkins, he was still trying to shake the habit of being his own boss and answering to no one but himself. But he knew enough about Jack Jenkins to realize he was walking on thin ice.

"They will take one look at this room, and the first name on their lips will be Hannibal's," said Jenkins. "And they know that Hannibal does my bidding. Even if they can't prove it."

Finch looked down at Grady, sprawled at his feet, out cold. He was a hard man, but there was still a tattered shred or two of decency in him, and he felt sorry for the boy.

"I reckon you want the boy dead too," he rasped. "Let me do it."

"You want to deny Hannibal his pleasure?"

Finch glared at the mulatto. He told himself that if he ever got the chance, he would put a bullet in Hannibal's brainpan. He was a very good shot; one chance was all he would need. It wasn't because Hannibal was a killer. It was because the mulatto was a homicidal maniac. Finch's resolve was purely an instinct for self-preservation. No one on this earth—and especially no striker—was safe as long as Hannibal lived.

"Call it the way you see it," said Finch, demonstrating cool courage.

"As I said, no shooting," replied Jenkins. "Bring him around. I want to know more about what he saw on the *Sultana.*"

"Wait just a minute," said Finch, in disbelief. "Sounds like you're aiming to go ahead with this thing."

Jenkins reached behind him to pick the lantern up off the floor. He set it on the table in front of him. He took a "long nine" cigar out of a coat pocket, bit off the tip, and lit the other end with a lucifer flicked to life on a thumbnail.

Now that the lantern stood on the table, Finch could see Jenkins clearly. He knew, of course, what his boss looked like. Even though this was the first time he had been chosen to ride with Jenkins on one of Jenkins's rare excursions from the "camp," Finch had been confronted by the man they called the Corpse Maker one-on-one when he had joined the strikers, and on a couple of other occasions during his three months with the gang. Still, face-to-face, at close range, Jenkins's physical presence never failed to impress him.

Though his build was powerful, Jenkins's head still seemed large for his body. The forehead was high, the strong jaw flared like the prow of a warship. The mouth was thin and straight, the nose aquiline, the piercing china-blue eyes small and set wide apart. As a whole these features were too small for the face. The flat brown cheeks were blue-shadowed; even though Jenkins was meticulous when it came to keeping himself clean-shaven, he always appeared to need a shave. His hair was the color of mahogany, brushed straight back, long at the collar, with patches of snow white at the temples.

From what Finch had heard Jack Jenkins had to be at least fifty years old, but he didn't look it. He was built like a pugilist, wide across the chest and shoulders, the muscles on his arms threatening to rip the fabric of the frock coat he wore. When he moved, he reminded Finch of the panther common in the woodlands and swamps of this part of the country.

Finch had been warned that Jenkins had no match with knife or gun. A shootist of some repute, and no little conceit, Finch wondered if Jenkins could match him with pistols, but not enough to put it to the test. He had seen firsthand evidence of the man's prowess in hand-to-hand combat. In his first week at the camp Finch had learned why five hundred tough, lawless men bent themselves to Jenkins's will. A striker had broken the rules, robbing and killing a lone traveler on a remote stretch of road. It had been bad enough that Jenkins had not approved the crime. Worse, the striker had tried to keep it secret, in order to avoid sharing the proceeds with Jenkins.

The culprit had been sentenced to death, but Jenkins had given him a fighting chance. He had been every bit as big and strong as Jenkins, but he hadn't lasted five minutes. Jenkins had snapped his neck like a dry twig.

Now, watching the blue cigar smoke curl overhead, Jenkins asked, "And why shouldn't we go ahead?"

"Because they'll be ready for us. Hannibal said that man in black probably overheard every word said about the plan by Blacky and Sikes."

"Most probably."

"So it would be crazy to go through with it."

"Not at all." Jenkins was willing to permit Finch's playing devil's advocate, as it gave him the opportunity to demonstrate his cunning—an opportunity no egomaniac could squander. "There are several strong arguments for proceeding as planned. First, to go on would be the last thing we would be expected to do. They will assume we'll decide to call off the attempt, now that the element of surprise has been lost. That would be logical. So, you see, in fact we recapture the element of surprise by doing the unexpected.

"Secondly, we must keep in mind the fact that the skipper of the *Sultana* is one Ezra Blake. Captain Blake is a veteran of the war. His service in the United States Navy was undistinguished. But to hear him tell it he was a hero, a master strategist." Jenkins smirked, rolling the cigar between teeth as square and white as marble headstones. "The truth is, he's a pompous, narrow-minded half-wit, and he will never accept the notion that a band of no-account scurvy dogs like us would even dare try to take the boat.

"The third reason is Sikes. I do not trust him to abide by his oath. I took a risk involving him in this scheme. I did so because he was a river pilot, and so seemed ideally suited for the task I laid out for him."

"But this boy said there were very few first-class passengers aboard the boat," said Finch.

"The *Sultana* cost almost a quarter of a million dollars to build. We'll strip her down to the bone. The boat has always been the principal target. What we might glean from the pockets of the passengers, or the mailbags she carries upriver, won't be a fraction of the loot we take off the boat itself. We'll sell it all, and at a handsome price, every last painting and piece of silverware, to New Orleans merchants. Those unscrupulous gentlemen have proved they would deal with the devil himself if it meant a profit. Their kind did business with Lafitte for many years. They have done business with me. Besides, the men have been chosen, the boats have been made ready. And I have an ace-in-the-hole."

"What?" asked Finch. "What do you mean?"

Jenkins smiled like a fox who has found a way into the chicken coop.

"The secret to success is flexibility. You must be prepared for every eventuality. You must foresee, and be able to counter, every possible problem that could arise. Let it suffice to say that I have another man already aboard the *Sultana*. He is in place precisely because I knew there was a risk involved in employing Sikes."

"I'll be damned," said Finch, impressed.

"Undoubtedly. As will we all."

"So we go ahead," said Hannibal. "But who will lead? Blacky is dead."

"I will," said Jenkins.

"You?" Finch was shocked. Jenkins never took an active role in carrying out the crimes he planned so brilliantly.

Jenkins nodded. "This will go down in history as the crime of the century, so I feel obliged to. Blacky was the only man I trusted with such responsibility. Besides, there won't be any survivors to bear witness against me."

"There is another reason, maybe," said Hannibal.

"You have your lucid moments, don't you, my blood-thirsty friend?"

"What are you talking about?" asked Finch, completely baffled.

"The man in black," said the mulatto.

"I must confess," said Jenkins, "that my curiosity has been aroused. I do want to meet the man who could kill Blacky and fight you, Hannibal, to a draw. Whoever he is, he will be a most worthy opponent for me."

C H A P T E R

17

Torn spent the balance of the day in the *Sultana*'s pilot-house, watching Duke Doniphan ply his trade. The ever-changing Mississippi was a constant challenge for pilots. Doniphan was clearly up to the task. It was a pleasure watching professionals work.

Because of the drought the river had dropped almost ten feet, and that fact alone created all kinds of hazards a pilot had to overcome. With the river so low, the side-wheeler was often drawing all the water in the channel. Leadsmen were constantly at work, and their lusty sing-song from port and starboard bow rang loud and clear over the pulse of the engines and the splash of the wheels.

Port lead: "Deep four!"

Starboard lead: "Mark three . . . Quarter less three . . ."

Port lead: "Mark three!"

Starboard lead: "Half twain! Quarter twain!"

And Doniphan would steer the boat a little to port, and deeper water.

Starboard lead: "Mark three . . . Mark three . . ."

Port lead: "Deep four!"

Starboard lead: "Deep four!"

And just when Torn thought he could relax . . .

Port lead: "Quarter less three! Mark twain!"

Starboard lead: "Mark three!"

Port lead: "Quarter less twain!"

And Doniphan would spin the wheel and pull her down to starboard, without a second to waste.

After an hour or so of this Torn doubted if he would have the steel nerve required to do the job Doniphan was doing. A pilot's decisions had to be swift and correct —there was precious little margin for error.

In particularly bad places the river had to be sounded. Early that afternoon Doniphan spotted a shoal crossing ahead. He took the side-wheeler to shore. A rowboat was put into the water with a picked crew aboard, and proceeded into the shoal. Many of the passengers lined the railings to observe its progress. Captain Blake did likewise from the hurricane deck, and Doniphan watched with the aid of a spyglass, which he considerately shared with Torn.

One of the *Sultana*'s mates was in charge of the "sounding boat," and it was he who used a twelve-foot pole to plumb the depths of the shoal in an attempt to find the "best water." When this was found, a buoy was put in place. The buoy was a board, five feet long, with a smaller board, painted bright yellow, standing up at right angles to the first, and the whole weighed down with heavy bricks at the end of stout rope, serving as an anchor.

With the buoy in place the mate took the precaution of sounding the water higher up and lower down. Failing to find better water, he gave the order for the rowboat's crew to ship their oars and hold them straight up in the air. Seeing this signal, Doniphan pulled a rope and released a shrill blast of steam from the side-wheeler's whistle. While the rowboat returned to the buoy Doniphan communicated his wishes to the engine room through a speaking tube. The *Sultana* crept forward. Down below on the boiler deck firemen bent their backs to feed the hungry boilers and build up steam. Doniphan steered straight for the buoy, and just at the right moment yelled "Full speed ahead!" into the speaking tube. As the side-wheeler churned forward to grind across the reef at full steam, the men in the rowboat bent to their oars to get out of the way. For a moment all involved held their collective breath; if the *Sultana* were to "strike and swing"—run aground—it would take hours, perhaps days, to spar her off.

But the side-wheeler plowed through, smashing the buoy into kindling, and reaching above the shoal. The speed was cut, the rowboat and crew brought back aboard, and Torn was reassured that the side-wheeler was indeed in the capable hands of a "lightning pilot."

Doniphan could read the river like the back of his hand. For Torn's edification he pointed out the slanting mark on the surface that indicated the presence of a bluff reef—"a steamboat killer if I ever seen one"—and a patch of "boiling" water where a sandbar was being eroded by shifting current and a new channel was being born. Torn learned that a river pilot was part prophet; Doniphan looked askance at an old dead oak leaning precariously out over the water on the eastern bank and declared that by next winter there would be a new snag blocking the channel here.

Duke shared the piloting duties on the *Sultana* with another knight of the tiller, a pale-skinned, red-haired giant named Quinn. They manned the wheel six hours on and six hours off. When Doniphan's shift drew to a close, Quinn came clomping up the pilothouse guy singing a bawdy song about a woman of dubious morals by the name of Miss Mabel Grand. He threw the door open, glowered belligerently at Torn, and then advanced with two-fisted menace on Doniphan, who was half his size. For one confused moment Torn thought there was going to be bloodshed.

"Unhand that wheel, you little runt! Let a real man take over. By God, a minute ago I thought you were killing this boat."

"Shoal," said Doniphan, unfazed. "A good thing I was up here at the time and not you, or we'd all be breathing water."

Quinn grunted, as though he'd been punched in the breadbasket. "You obviously don't know who you're talking to, half-pint. My father was a hurricane and my mother was an avalanche. I was raised on rattlesnake milk. Most mornings I eat a dozen alligators for breakfast, and wash the critters down with a barrel of busthead whiskey. Don't rile me, little man, 'cause I'm calamity's child."

"I will agree," said Doniphan, with infuriating drollery, "that when you were born, a calamity did occur."

Quinn gnashed his teeth and snarled, "I've been known to punch my way straight through the middle of a mountain with these here fists, and when I raise my voice in anger, even thunder gives up and goes home. I have a constitution made of boiler iron, and my heart is petrified wood. Blood is my favorite drink, and desolation is my favorite pastime. The riders of the Apocalypse are my drinkin' buddies, and the devil himself asks me for advice."

Torn relaxed. Quinn was waving his big fists and looking fierce, but it was apparent now that this was some kind of ritual. He was a bona fide riverman—the Mississippi had sired many like him: heavy drinkers, fierce fighters, prodigious braggarts, two-legged profanity mills. But for all that they were good men, most of them brave, stoic, and true.

Doniphan appeared blissfully unconcerned by the ferocious giant looming over him. He checked his pocket watch, gave the bell rope two tugs, followed by two more, and then let go of the wheel. He turned to the cub, who was warily watching Quinn out of the corner of his eye.

"Don't pay this blowhard any mind, boy. Whatever he tries to teach you about piloting, forget it, because it's all wrong. He can't tell a sawyer from a wind reef, and it just proves that God has a soft spot in His heart for empty-headed fools that he hasn't killed every boat on the river."

Quinn growled like a riled grizzly bear. "One day, Doniphan, I swear, I'll bathe in your blood."

Doniphan grinned and left the pilothouse, accompanied by Torn. "Quinn was raised on a keelboat," said Duke.

"I guessed as much."

"He knows the river. But better than that he knows how to fight."

"You're pretty sure Jenkins will try to take this boat."

Doniphan nodded. "And I've been giving it a lot of thought. Trying to guess where he might make his move. I think it'll be above Memphis."

"Why?"

"Islands Thirty-seven and Twenty-six, a lot of tow-heads and dry bars. Any number of places where the channels are narrow and shallow, and we won't be able to use our speed."

Torn nodded. "I've been giving it some thought too. The first thing we do is secure the safety of the passengers."

"How do you propose to do that?"

"Get them off this boat. Then we'll arm the crew and . . ."

Doniphan was shaking his head vigorously. "One big problem. Captain Blake."

"I'll handle Blake."

"You'll have another fight on your hands, Judge. An ex-Confederate using federal authority to commandeer his boat?" Doniphan whistled. "We'll have the gol-durn Civil War all over again."

CHAPTER 18

Duke Doniphan insisted on getting a closer look at Sikes. Torn agreed, with reservations, expecting the confrontation to turn ugly. The pilot looked like a man with a very big chip on his shoulder.

On the starboard promenade of the boiler deck, as they made their way to the Kentucky stateroom, they met the Ashbrooks. Rebecca looked as beautiful as ever in an elegant dress of blue organdy with a matching parasol. She appeared very pleased to see Torn. The same could not be said for John Raleigh Ashbrook. But he was too much the gentleman, or too committed to the role he was playing, not to pause and make polite conversation.

"How are your hands, my friend?" he asked Torn.

"Fine, thanks to your daughter."

"What?"

Torn could have kicked himself.

Rebecca nimbly swept them past Torn's faux pas. "Those bandages should be changed, Mr. Torn."

He was relieved to see that her eyes were laughing. "Yes, ma'am."

"We have been invited to dine with the captain this evening," she said. "Will you be joining us?"

"I doubt it. Captain Blake seems to bear strong prejudice toward those of us who served in the Confederate army."

"But not against Southerners in general, apparently," remarked Ashbrook.

"A distinction he's forced to make," surmised Torn. "After all, he is the skipper of a packet which trades at Southern river ports. He has to deal with Southern merchants."

"And put up with a Southern pilot." Doniphan grinned. "A soldier doesn't make war against civilians. And the captain is still making war."

"My word," said Ashbrook. "He seemed cordial enough."

"People aren't always what they seem," said Torn.

Ashbrook shifted his weight from one foot to the other.

"Father is escorting me to the ladies' cabin," announced Rebecca, a fact that clearly vexed her. "While he goes off to the main saloon to have a drink and play cards. Neither of which he ought to do."

"Now, Rebecca," scolded Ashbrook, with an apologetic smile at Torn and Doniphan. "My daughter is too outspoken."

"Nonsense," said Rebecca. "I have to look out for you if you won't look out for yourself."

"Forgive us, gentlemen," said Ashbrook, taking her

by the arm and steering her past Torn and the side-wheeler's pilot. "We must be going."

As they passed, Torn touched his hat brim to her. She answered the gesture with a warm smile, and with something like clairvoyance as well as sympathy in a gaze that was somehow shy and saucy at the same time. Her glance seemed to say that she knew what he was feeling toward her, and what the future held in store for them both. To that degree, at that moment, she seemed wise beyond her years.

"A lovely lady," remarked Doniphan once the Ash-brooks were out of earshot. "I venture to say she's set her cap for you, Judge."

"Stick to piloting," admonished Torn, looking stern, but secretly pleased.

Arriving at the Kentucky stateroom, they found a burly roustabout who said his name was Bledsoe and had taken over the job of watching Sikes for the first mate, Harker.

"The cap'n wants a guard on this man round the clock," explained Bledsoe. "I took over for Mr. Harker, and I'll be just outside the door if you need me."

Torn nodded. Apparently he had no say in the matter, so he said nothing. Captain Blake was within his rights to take whatever steps he deemed necessary for the safety of his ship and passengers.

Doniphan took one glance at Sikes and nodded emphatically. "That's him. That's the sorry bastard who sank the *Tuscarora*."

The pilot's cheeks were mottled with anger. He looked as though all he wanted out of life was the chance to get his hands around the striker's throat. Torn counted them all lucky that Duke wasn't "heeled."

For his part Sikes tried to act as though he didn't know Doniphan from Adam, but the stark fear glittering in his eyes testified otherwise. "He's crazy! I don't know what he's talking about. Keep him away from me!"

"You're going to hang," snarled Doniphan, venom dripping from every word. "You got away once, but you won't escape justice a second time, unless it's over my dead body. I'm going to tell it the way it happened, and I'll count myself the luckiest man on God's good green earth if they'll let me be the one to spring the trapdoor on your gallows."

With that malicious promise ringing in the air Doniphan stormed out.

"Cut me a deal, Judge," rasped Sikes, a sob caught in his throat. "Swear I won't hang and I'll lead you to Jenkins's camp. I know right where it is."

Torn shook his head. "Things have changed. In your case for the worse. I didn't know before that you were responsible for the deaths of those innocent people who perished when the *Tuscarora* sank. If the jury finds you guilty, you're going to hang."

And this time, he thought, I won't lose any sleep over it.

"But you want Jenkins!" cried Sikes in despair.

The striker was sweating, but Torn's smile chilled him to the marrow in his bones.

"I think I've got him already," said Torn.

CHAPTER

19

SINCE CAPTAIN BLAKE HAD TAKEN UPON HIMSELF THE RESPONSIbility for Sikes, Torn left his prisoner for the roustabout named Bledsoe to guard and headed for the dining room to get some supper.

The *Sultana*'s dining room was downright opulent, with chandeliers, damask walls, gilded mirrors, and oils depicting misty river scenes in ornate frames. The bone china and silverware were imported and of the highest quality. Torn couldn't help but wonder how much Jack Jenkins might fetch on the black market for these table settings alone.

The food was outstanding. The side-wheeler's chef was a man of considerable repute, recruited from the best restaurant in New Orleans, if the steward who waited on Torn was to be believed. The menu was an extraordinary reading experience. Torn had to deliberate a long time before opting for roast quail with an orange glaze, accompanied by stewed tomatoes and spinach with cream, preceded by turtle soup, and capped off with plum pudding, coffee, and cognac.

Torn had a theory that these rich trappings were essential to the survival of the riverboat business. Traveling on a riverboat was a risky enterprise, always had been. Few boats "died" of old age. Most were sunk as a result of pilot error or boiler explosion. First-class passengers were lured by all this extravagance, which was meant to offset the risk.

It proved to be a nostalgic dining experience for Torn, bringing back vivid memories of family dinners at Ravenoak. In the years since, his constitution had adapted to army rations, prison-camp slop, and then rough frontier "bait," so that by the time he had finished with the *Sultana*'s rich fare, he was almost sick to his stomach.

The long dining room remained virtually empty while he was there: an older couple, and a younger, two gentlemen dining alone. Torn was convinced that the only reason Jenkins would risk assaulting the side-wheeler, when there were so few pockets aboard worth picking, was that the old Corpse Maker intended to strip this floating palace to the bare bones. Not that Jenkins himself would take any risks. He had a host of strikers to carry out his criminal undertakings.

Torn resolved to speak to Captain Blake tonight. Duke Doniphan was confident that Jenkins would not strike until they were above Memphis, but Torn didn't feel like taking chances with the lives of innocents. He knew he would have a fight on his hands when he told the side-wheeler's skipper of his plan. Blake would be uncooperative. And in that case Torn would have to use federal authority, which was supreme on inland water-ways.

As he dawdled over the after-dinner cognac, preparing for his battle royal with Blake, he felt a change in the tempo of the *Sultana*'s big wheels. The steward informed him that they were approaching Vicksburg, where they would remain until morning—to proceed at night, with the river so low, was too dangerous.

Torn ventured out onto the boiler deck's starboard promenade, joining other spectators. He saw the lights of the city, high on the commanding bluffs, off the starboard bow. Here, the river had once been serpentine; a cutoff had reduced seventy miles of Mississippi River down to thirty. The cutoff had ended the riverport career of Vicksburg's sister city, Delta, a fate similar to that which had befallen Hard Times.

Vicksburg had suffered as well. A big island and a shallow secondary channel, without sufficient current unless the river rose to flood level, stood between the city and the river these days. With the river so low the channel was little more than a mudflat now. Wharf boats had been secured below the city, and it was to one of these that the *Sultana* made fast.

A cabin boy came down the promenade to inform everyone that the side-wheeler would remain here until morning, and that if anyone wished to indulge in a nocturnal visit to the city, carriages were always available ashore to take them there.

There was a great deal of coming and going on the stages joining the steamboat to the wharf boat, bow and stern. Lanterns and torches hurled back the muggy darkness of the moonless night. The mosquitoes were ferocious. Torn could look down on this frenzy of activity from the relative calm of the promenade, but he could not escape the swarm of insects.

He had no desire to visit Vicksburg. He had been there before. Even now, twelve years after the famous siege that had won the river for the Union and broken the back of the Confederacy, the city bore many scars of that six-week ordeal. Torn had been fighting in the east during the siege in '63—marching north with Lee's Army of North Virginia, in that ill-fated invasion of the North—to meet a terrible fate of his own at Gettysburg. But he knew the story of the siege well.

Twenty-seven thousand soldiers and three thousand civilians, huddling behind earthworks and taking refuge in the caves that still honeycombed the hills, had been mercilessly bombarded by federal gunboats and land batteries. The Union cannon had reduced much of the city to rubble. Famine and disease had been Yankee allies. The siege was a testament to the tremendous valor on both sides, the scarred city a testament to courage, but Torn could think only of the terrible suffering and loss of life. There was no glory in war, only pain and suffering and heartbreak. The city was a poignant reminder of the war, and thinking of the war reminded him of Melony Hancock. He felt the cold, sharp claws of loneliness tearing at his soul.

He had prowled Vicksburg's streets in search of her, as he had roamed the streets of many towns and cities, and traveled many roads, all in vain. Countless empty miles and empty nights. He was reaching for the daguerreotype of his fiancée, which rested in the pocket of his frock coat against his heart, when he saw Rebecca Ashbrook hurrying up the promenade, visibly upset.

"What's wrong?" he asked.

"You must come quickly. My father . . . oh, you're the only one I can turn to."

"What happened?"

"Please. I fear for his life."

"Lead the way," said Torn.

CHAPTER

20

REBECCA TOOK HIM TO THE VERMONT STATEROOM, LOCATED ON the port side of the boiler deck.

John Raleigh Ashbrook was slumped in a chair, head in hands, the portrait of despair. When he saw Torn, he jumped to his feet, white as a boiled shirt.

"Rebecca!" he gasped. "What have you done?"

"He's the only one who can help us, Father."

"No! No, don't you realize—"

"If you won't tell him, I will."

"Are you in some kind of danger?" asked Torn, bewildered.

Ashbrook sank back into the chair, as though he did not have the strength to stand. "I have made a terrible blunder, sir," he moaned wretchedly.

"I'm listening."

Ashbrook sighed. "I am a dead man. Who will look after my dear child, sir, when I'm gone? She has no one else in this world."

Torn didn't like mysteries. "Stop feeling sorry for yourself," he snapped, "and tell me what happened."

Even though Ashbrook was in the depths of despair, his pride was wounded by Torn's bluntness. He waxed indignant. "You have no right—"

"I will tell him, since you won't," said Rebecca. "And remember, Father, I warned you against playing cards." She turned to Torn. "My father is not a very good card-player. He was certainly no match for this man Tyree."

"Tyree?"

"A professional gambler, apparently," said Ashbrook dismally. "Of course I had no inkling at first. I never would have—"

"No," said Torn wryly. "They don't generally adver-tise the fact. All their potential marks would scatter like quail. There's at least one cardsharp on every steam-boat. You can bank on that. How much did you lose?"

"Everything," groaned Ashbrook. "Everything."

Torn's eyes narrowed. He was getting suspicious of John Raleigh Ashbrook all over again. Was this crisis genuine, or just another confidence game? Was Ash-brook in the process of trying to milk money out of him? If so, Rebecca was taking an active part in this artful dodge, using her feminine wiles to lure him into the trap, sensing—as women always could—that here was a man captivated by her charms.

"So you're cleaned out," said Torn.

His tone was cynical. Rebecca's eyes flashed anger. She seemed to know exactly what he was thinking.

"Tyree took it all," said Ashbrook. "And more than just money. He won all the ore samples. And . . . and a share in the mine."

Torn was incredulous. "You bet your samples and a share in the mine on a hand of poker?"

"Not just any hand, sir. Three aces. How could I lose?"

"You can always lose. What was the game?"

"Draw. I was dealt the three aces. Tyree drew three cards."

"And he beat three aces?"

"He had a full house. How could he draw three cards to a full house? What are the odds?"

"Pretty steep I'd say," murmured Torn. "Tyree was dealing?"

"Yes! He must have cheated, sir. He must have."

"But why do you say you're a dead man?"

Ashbrook threw an apprehensive look in Rebecca's direction.

"You must tell him," she said. "What choice do you have?"

John Raleigh Ashbrook was a beaten man in every sense of the word. "Very well," he said, his voice a croak. "The ore samples are genuine. But the mine from which they came is not on my property. No such mine exists. And when this man Tyree discovers he owns a share in a mine which does not exist . . . well, what do you think he will do?"

Torn could see the irony in the situation. "And you complain that he cheated you? A thief crying thief."

"You can look down your nose at us if you wish, Mr. Torn," snapped Rebecca, leaping to her father's defense. "But I think you would have to walk in my father's shoes before you are qualified to judge him."

Torn was mollifed. "Maybe so. I'll see what I can do. If Tyree is a cheat, and I can prove it, whatever he took from you is still yours. But after this is resolved, Mr. Ashbrook, you will answer to the law. You will answer to me."

With that he left the stateroom, still feeling the sting of Rebecca's reprimand.

She caught up with him on the promenade. "What will you do?" she asked.

"I don't know yet." This was all he needed: something else to worry about, at a time when he had his hands full worrying about Jack Jenkins.

"Father told me Tyree said he intended to go into Vicksburg to have the samples assayed."

Torn nodded and started to turn away.

She reached out and put a hand on his arm, and he forgot all about Jenkins. Lanterns had been lighted on the promenade, and their soft golden touch on her hair, and that faint fragrance of jasmine, completely beguiled him.

"I apologize for speaking so sharply," she said. "You're right, of course. Only I . . ."

"I'm the one who should apologize. True or not I had no right to say it."

"He isn't a bad man. But life has made him bitter. Life makes you do things you wouldn't do if you had a choice. The Yankees took away his property, and the land he found in Mexico proved to be worthless. He fell in with bad company. There was a man in Vera Cruz, who gave him the ore samples for a half share in the proceeds. It was this man who came up with the idea of my father returning to the States and finding individuals gullible enough to invest in a mine they would never even bother trying to see."

Torn nodded. "Unfortunately a lot of people are that gullible."

"I tried to talk Father out of it. But I failed. I couldn't very well abandon him. He needs me. He's desperate. He doesn't want money for himself. He wants to provide for me. He is ashamed that he has nothing of value to leave me. I can't make him understand that I don't want anything bought at the price of his integrity. He is so desperate that even when he discovered you were a federal judge, he decided to continue on to St. Louis. He has corresponded with men there who have expressed a keen interest in investing."

"You told him I was a judge."

"Of course. I told him you were suspicious. I could tell that you were. I was hoping to persuade him to forget this dishonest scheme." She sighed. "I know what you must think of me. I'm not trying to defend myself. I only wish you could understand."

"I do. You are standing by your father, and standing up for him, and I admire you for that."

"Do you, really?"

"Yes," said Torn, fighting the urge to take her in his arms and kiss those full, red, slightly parted lips that beckoned him. "I admire you more than I should."

He pulled away, turned sharply on his heel, and beat a hasty retreat.

CHAPTER 21

RETURNING TO HIS STATEROOM, TORN DISCOVERED THAT Harker, the *Sultana*'s first mate, had joined Bledsoe.

"I come to take over watching the prisoner, Judge," said Harker, throwing a knuckle salute at Torn, "so's Bledsoe can get some vittles."

"Before you do, I'd like a word with you, privately." Torn turned to Bledsoe. "Do you mind staying on here a little while longer?"

"Fine with me, Judge." Bledsoe had precious few opportunities to enjoy the plush comforts of a stateroom.

Torn took Harker out onto the promenade. "I'm looking for a man named Tyree. Know him?"

Harker scowled. "That I do. A cardsharp, Tyree is. Spends a lot of time on this boat."

Torn got the impression that Tyree was very low on the first mate's list of favorite people and surmised that at some point in time Harker might have lost a portion of his wages at Tyree's table.

109

"Which stateroom is his?"

"The Maryland. Right down here."

Harker led the way down the starboard promenade.

Torn knocked on the louvered door. Rebecca had said the gambler's expressed intention was to go into Vicksburg, but Torn had no way of knowing whether or not Tyree had already disembarked.

A cabin boy, toting a pair of hand-tooled Middleton half boots polished to a high shine, passed by. Harker snagged him by the arm.

"Have you seen the gambler, boy?"

The cabin boy nodded. "Yassuh. Mistuh Tyree done gone ashore."

The first mate let the boy go on about his errands. "There you have it, Judge. The gentleman has gone to Vicksburg." He doused the "gentleman" with plenty of sarcasm. "Probably looking for better pickings than he found aboard."

Torn nodded. "I'm going to search his room, Mr. Harker. Do you have any objections?"

"Well, I should have, shouldn't I?" Harker grinned ear to ear. "But you're a judge, after all, so I reckon it'll be all right." He leaned closer and winked like a conspirator. "I'll just wait around out here and keep a sharp lookout."

Torn smiled. "Obliged."

"Oh, no need to thank me. I owe Mr. Tyree that much and more."

Torn turned the latch and slipped inside. The stateroom was dark, but just enough lantern light from the promenade filtered through the door's louvers to aid him in finding a Rochester hand lamp. Torn carried a waterproof match case; from this he took a "strike anywhere" and scratched it to life with his thumbnail. He lighted the lamp and turned it down low.

He found what he was looking for under the bed—a valise of handsome Russian leather. It was locked. Torn hesitated a moment, then used the saber-knife to slice the heavy lock flap. His conscience would bother him if Tyree turned out to be completely honest. But he thought the odds against that were extremely high.

He was right.

Torn had met a lot of gamblers in his time. They were thick as fleas on a redbone hound out on the frontier. Some were honest, relying on their skill. Most, though, resorted to some method of trickery, balancing the risk of exposure—with its dire consequences—against an overwhelming advantage at the table. Many of them were masters of the false cut and false shuffle, the second deal and bottom deal. But there were those who relied on "mechanics" to give them the edge.

Tyree was in the latter category. The valise contained a card trimmer, a corner rounder, and a card pricker.

The trimmer was a device fashioned from brass and steel, with an attached blade fitted with an ivory handle. It had a legitimate use: trimming the frayed edges from a much-used deck. But Torn had a hunch Tyree used it to "shave" certain cards, making them easy to detect while shuffling and dealing.

The corner rounder was a device similar in appearance and manufacture to the card trimmer. It, too, could be employed legitimately, to cut new corners on an old deck. But it could also mark particular cards by altering their corners.

The brass card pricker pierced a card with a tiny needle, making marks that the unsuspecting would not discern, but that an accomplished sharp could read in the same way a blind person read braille. A dealer could identify by these bumps every card passing through his hands.

"This man," murmured Torn, "is as crooked as a dog's leg."

He carefully examined a few of the decks held fast in inside pockets of the valise. He found a brand-new deck still wearing the E. N. Grandine paper wrapper. Torn was convinced these cards were "readers." Although Grandine made honest decks, he had gained some notoriety for producing and advertising marked decks. The navy-blue backs of the cards in this deck were covered with tiny white symbols. Torn noticed that the same two symbols, a Y and a crescent, were to be found at the top right of every card. While all the other symbols remained the same from one card to the next, these two symbols moved through a series of distinctly different positions, denoting the different face values of the cards.

Torn found another deck that had been marked with the card pricker. Two more decks had "line and scroll" work, which shaded the various decorations on the back so subtly that only the crooked cardsharp would know what to look for.

It surprised Torn that Tyree had risked leaving all this incriminating evidence behind. Then he remembered that Tyree had Ashbrook's sample case in his possession. The gambler would have his hands full with that case. He had taken a chance, leaving this valise unattended, but then gamblers had the nerve to take such chances. If exposed, he could argue that all the devices, save the card pricker, could be employed in a honest fashion.

Torn took a lot of time studying the decks—so much, in fact, that Harker came in to make sure all was well.

The first mate's features turned ugly when he saw Tyree's devices. "By God, the sorry son of a bitch ought to be keelhauled," growled Harker, grinding his teeth.

"I take it you lost some money to the man."

"A couple months' wages if I lost a bit. And I ain't the only fool in the crew to make the mistake of trying his luck at Tyree's table. I see now that luck had nothing to do with it. Wait until I get my hands around his neck."

"Calm down," said Torn. "I want to arrange a warm reception for Tyree if he comes back aboard."

"Say the word, Judge. I'm your man."

"Here's what I want you to do. . . ."

CHAPTER 22

THE ROCKAWAY CARRIAGE TOOK THE GAMBLER TYREE UP WASH-
ington Street past the old docks and turned east into the
heart of Vicksburg on Clay Street. Several times Tyree
consulted his keywinder by the frail light of the small
inside lantern, and several times he leaned out to exhort
the rockaway's driver to make better speed. The driver
was eager to please, but he could not coax the pair of
swayback nags in the traces into a quicker gait. They
were old and set in their ways, apologized the driver.
Their ironshod hooves clacked and clattered on the cob-
blestones in a rhythm far too leisurely for Tyree's taste.

He was ordinarily a man of remarkable patience and
self-discipline—qualities a man who made a living as he
did needed to possess. But tonight he was obligated to
report to someone—he didn't know who—who would
be, according to Jenkins's plan, waiting for him at the
corner of Cherry and Jackson streets. As the length of
the *Sultana*'s stops was a factor beyond even Jenkins's

control, this someone would have been waiting last night, and would be waiting tomorrow night as well, until ten o' clock. It was getting late, and Tyree didn't want to miss the rendezvous. He wanted to get this whole distasteful business over with.

Tyree was a lean, darkly handsome man who had remained fit despite his nearly forty years. His complexion was pale, his features angular. As always he was well dressed in a respectable dark blue broadcloth, and was meticulously well groomed. A vain man, he paid a great deal of attention to his appearance. But the evening was hot and muggy, and his ruffled-front linen shirt was soaked with sweat and stuck uncomfortably to his skin. That annoyed him.

What annoyed him even more was the fact that he had to be at this rendezvous when what he really wanted was to get the ore samples, in the case on the seat beside him, to an assayer as soon as possible.

But he didn't dare let Jack Jenkins down.

Somehow he had to dissociate himself from Jenkins. Maybe he would head west. Or better yet, go down to Mexico, now that he was part owner of what he was sure would prove to be an incredibly rich silver mine.

Tyree smiled. His luck was finally turning. He'd hit the jackpot with that old fool Ashbrook. He was going to be filthy rich. Rich enough to get so far away that Jenkins would never find him.

That was the key. The Corpse Maker thinks he owns me, thought Tyree angrily. Just because I made a mistake with that woman in New Orleans, and he got me out of it, and then made me swear to that striker's oath. Once a striker, always a striker; once you had sold your soul to Jack Jenkins, he never surrendered title.

"We'll see," muttered Tyree.

Problem was, he was afraid of Jenkins. He didn't like to admit it to himself. But he could remember, vividly, what Jenkins's men had done to the woman's husband, years ago in the Crescent City. They hadn't just assassinated him. They'd cut him up into little bloody pieces. And it hadn't made the slightest difference to them or to Jenkins that the man had been one of the city's leading citizens.

Tyree had been working for Jenkins ever since. Somewhat like an indentured servant. For the most part he picked out wealthy travelers for the murderous attention of squads of strikers. The strikers usually traveled the steamboats as deck passengers, posing as itinerant laborers. They would disembark with the poor soul Tyree had marked. Marked for death. Tyree did no more than that, but that was quite enough to live with. He never took part in the robbing and killing and disposing of the bodies, but he carried the grim deeds on his conscience.

The rockaway turned left on Cherry Street, crossed China Street, then Grove, passed the Duff Green Mansion. The stately three-story house had been a hospital during the war, first for Confederate, then for Union, sick and wounded. It had scarcely been touched during the fierce Yankee bombardment of the siege of '63. Folks claimed that was a miracle.

Tyree had never put much stock in miracles—until Ashbrook had sat down at his table in the *Sultana*'s main saloon.

They rolled by the old courthouse, where U. S. Grant had raised the Stars and Stripes over the city he had ruthlessly reduced to rubble. A block farther and the

rockaway stopped. Tyree got out, carrying the sample
case, paid the fare, and took a careful look around as the
carriage drove on, turning at the corner onto Main to
head back toward the levee.

Just up the street was the Balfour House, a magnificent Greek Revival mansion that had been home to
Emma Balfour, famous for the moving diary she had
written during the siege. The mansion had served as
Union headquarters after the fall of the city. Tonight it
was the scene of a soiree. The street and private drive
were lined with conveyances of every description. The
mansion was ablaze with light. Men and women in elegant evening dress passed in and out through the front
doors. The sweet strains of a waltz reached across the
night to tantalize Tyree. The gambler looked longingly
in the direction of the music. He had promised himself
long ago that one day he would gain entry into high
society. He felt as though he belonged there. The circumstances of his birth, though, had conspired to lead
him down a less respectable road. Now, thanks to Ashbrook, he was standing on the threshold of realizing his
dream.

"Tyree."

The gambler whirled, almost tripping over the sample
case he had set down on the pavement beside him.

A scrofulous old veteran stood before him. He wore a
moth-eaten tunic of butternut gray. A forage cap was
pulled low over his face, and a scraggly beard concealed
his features. He smelled like a sewer rat. Tyree hadn't
heard the man slip up behind him.

"Do I know you, sir?"

"Don't you recognize me?" The man lifted his head. A
thread of light from the gas lamps lining Cherry Street

reached under the bent bill of the forage cap. China-blue eyes fastened on Tyree's astonished face.

"Jenkins."

A soft chuckle. "Jack Jenkins is not welcome in Vicksburg. But who would molest an old soldier who gave his all for the Confederacy?"

"I didn't realize I would be meeting *you* here."

"I have decided to take an active part in this endeavor. I killed one horse and took the second to the brink just to get here before the *Sultana* arrived. If I didn't know you better, Tyree, I'd swear you weren't happy to see me."

Tyree was thinking about his weapons. He carried a four-barrel Sharps derringer, .22 caliber, in a coat pocket. Sheathed to his left forearm, under the sleeve, was a his "fifth ace," a dagger with a silver-studded handle of gutta-percha.

"I'll be pleased to get this business over with," he said. He was scared, but he didn't show it. He was running a bluff, something he knew how to do very well. His features were coldly impassive, his complexion as white as marble in the gaslight.

"There's been a new development," said Jenkins. "I am taking charge personally."

"I thought Blacky—"

"Blacky is indisposed. Another of my men is the prisoner of one of the *Sultana*'s passengers. A tall man, dressed in black. Perhaps you've seen him."

"You have made it my business to know all about the *Sultana*'s first-class passengers. I asked about that man. His name is Torn. He's a federal judge."

There was a gleam of bloodthirsty delight in Jenkins's eyes. "I've never killed a federal judge before."

"So his prisoner is one of yours," said Tyree.

"One of ours, you mean. Sikes, the pilot. When the time comes, we will free him."

Tyree had a hunch Jenkins meant to free Sikes from the mortal coils of life. "You say when the time comes. How will I know? You haven't seen fit to enlighten me. All I know is that your men will slip aboard and indulge in wholesale robbery and looting. I must appear to be one of the victims. I would be of no further use to you in the future if I am seen as your accomplice."

"Don't worry," said Jenkins. "No one will suspect you. This man—this Judge Torn—is aware of our plans. Have you seen anything to indicate as much?"

"Nothing," said Tyree, alarmed. "If we're found out, then why—"

"Because apparently the judge expects us to do the obvious. He doesn't think we will go through with the plan."

"That's not only obvious, but sensible."

Jenkins ignored this objection. He nudged the sample case with the toe of his boot. "What do we have here?"

Tyree's heart skipped a beat. He had been praying that Jenkins would pay no attention to the case, while knowing all along that nothing escaped this man's attention. He hadn't expected to meet Jenkins himself, and he'd been confident he could handle any curiosity a hireling might have displayed about the sample case.

Should he lie or be honest with Jenkins? It was a question with life-and-death consequences, and Tyree had to make the decision in a split second. Any hesitation would only ignite Jenkins's suspicious nature.

His nerve failed him. It was one bluff he didn't dare run. "Ore samples from a silver mine," he said, the bitter taste of defeat on his tongue. "One of the passengers, a fellow named Ashbrook, has a silver mine down in Mexico. I won the samples in a poker game. I didn't dare leave them aboard."

Jenkins was watching Tyree like a hawk. The gambler knew it couldn't be so, but it seemed as though the man could see right through him—could somehow know that he had been planning to break the striker's oath and make off with the silver. Jenkins reserved the right to a share of every striker's ill-gotten gains.

"We'll see to the silver later," said Jenkins, with a cold smile. "Tell me more about Ashbrook."

"I don't know much more. He's bound for St. Louis, looking for investors to finance the mining operation."

"He travels alone?"

"His daughter is with him. You're not going to take the samples now, are you?"

"Take them back to the *Sultana* with you. After all, we'll have to rob you along with the other passengers, won't we?"

"But I will get my share," said Tyree, almost choking on his resentment of Jenkins, and hating himself for being such a coward. But he consoled himself with the fact that Jenkins couldn't take away his share in the silver mine. The samples were lost, but that was only a couple of thousand dollars. Tyree just knew his position as a shareholder would prove to be worth a fortune.

"Of course you'll get your share." Jenkins chuckled. "I reward loyal service. And you are loyal—aren't you, Tyree?"

Tyree nodded.

"Then you may go."

The gambler hefted the sample case and started

down Cherry Street on foot. Jenkins turned the other way. At the corner of Main and Cherry he was joined by Finch.

"Do you trust that cheat?" asked Finch. "He could betray you once you're on the *Sultana.*"

Jenkins shrugged. "He may not see me board. And if he does, he won't have the guts. Oh, there is no doubt he would prefer to be rid of me. But his troubles will soon be over. The fool has no idea he is destined for the bottom of the river. You and Hannibal go on. The men are waiting at the boats." Jenkins grinned. "I'll see you tomorrow night—aboard the *Sultana.*"

CHAPTER

23

THE LAST PLACE TYREE WANTED TO GO WAS BACK TO THE *Sultana*. But he was trapped. He didn't see any way out of his predicament. He racked his brain trying to find a solution. Reaching the wharf boat, he hesitated crossing the stage to board the side-wheeler. He had the feeling that once he stepped aboard, he would never get off alive. Yet, like a condemned man going to his gallows, he had to make those steps. At least he could delay the inevitable by dallying on the wharf boat.

While he anguished in the shadows of the wharf boat promenade, staring at the *Sultana* much as a man would look, with morbid curiosity, at the coffin he knew he would be buried in, he saw Jenkins, one deck below, cross the stage. Jenkins was still wearing the old Confederate-soldier disguise.

The gambler was stunned. He was terrified of Jenkins, even more so after tonight's unexpected meeting with the old Corpse Maker—filled with the same fear and loathing any person would feel in the presence of a diamond-back rattler. He couldn't believe Jenkins would be so bold and couldn't imagine what sinister reason lay behind the man's boarding the side-wheeler.

Again he almost gave in to panic—almost turned and ran. But he had no real hope of escape, not anymore. At the same time he felt compelled to board the *Sultana* in a hurry. What if Jenkins looked for him? The man expected him to be there. What would happen if he wasn't? Tyree didn't want to wait and find out.

He watched until Jenkins disappeared into the melee of people, livestock, wagons, and freight on the main deck. Then he crossed the stage and slipped up to the boiler deck. In a hurry to reach the sanctuary of his stateroom, he hastened down the promenade and through the door. He dropped the sample case and groped through the darkness for the hand lamp.

When he lighted the lamp, he saw Torn sitting in a wing chair in the corner of the stateroom.

Tyree lunged for the door. He was quick, and might have reached the promenade, except that he stumbled over the sample case and almost fell flat on his face. This gave Torn time to catch him. Tyree wrenched away and reached for the Sharps derringer in his pocket.

Torn drew his Colt Peacemaker quicker than thought. He didn't have to see it to know that Tyree had a weapon and was going for it. Measuring the blow, he laid the Colt's six-inch barrel across Tyree's skull.

The gambler crumpled like a poleaxed steer. He blacked out for an instant. By the time he had regained consciousness, Torn had confiscated the Sharps as well as the razor-sharp fifth ace beneath his sleeve.

"Stand up," said Torn.

Tyree got as far as sitting up. He touched his head; the fingers came away sticky with blood. He blinked at the lights madly dancing behind his eyes and felt like throwing up. "My God," he mumbled, thick-tongued, "you've cracked my skull."

"Thought I might knock some sense into you. That was a fatal mistake you almost made."

"What do you think you're doing, bushwhacking me like that? You've got no right—"

"Think again." Torn took a step back and reached for the valise of Russian leather on the bed. He tipped it over. The trimmer, rounder, and card pricker spilled out, along with several decks of cards. "You're a cheat, Tyree. There's nothing I hate worse than a crooked tinhorn."

"I . . . I . . ." Tyree stared wide-eyed at the devices and lost all color. He knew that protests of innocence would gain him nothing.

"You know," said Torn, a steely edge to his casual tone of voice, "on the other side of the river they'd generally just get a rope and drape you by the neck from a tree. But I'm told that *on* the river they do it a little differently."

Keeping the Colt trained on Tyree, he circled to the stateroom door.

Harker stood outside, with three roustabouts who looked every bit as burly and bad-tempered as the first mate.

Stepping in, Harker glowered at Tyree and growled, "Grab him, boys."

The trio of deckhands surged forward. Tyree uttered a strangled cry as they snatched him up. One got him by the left arm. Another pinned his right. The third got around behind him and snaked an arm around his throat. Harker stepped in close, almost nose to nose, and there was nothing remotely friendly about his smile.

"You've shaved your last pasteboard, gambler."

Tyree made funny noises, eyes bulging out of their sockets.

"You ought to tell him what to expect," suggested Torn.

"With pleasure. Mr. Tyree, sir, us boys were all big losers at your table. Now I can't honestly say we like losing, but we can live with it if our pockets are cleaned out fair and square. But when you use dirty tricks to steal our hard-earned wages, well, that don't sit well."

Tyree gagged, clawing ineffectually at the arm crushing his windpipe.

"So the judge here has found you guilty," continued Harker, "and he's been kind enough to appoint us your executioners. Now, we could hang you from a railing, but the boys and me have decided to keelhaul you instead. In case you don't know what keelhauling is, let me tell you. We tie a rope around your ankles and another around your wrists. A nice long rope. Two of us will take one rope down the starboard side and two will take the other rope down the port, pulling you under the boat from bow to stern. We might have to do that a few times before we get the job done, but not a single one of us will complain, I'm sure. All I want to know, Tyree, is just how long can you hold your breath?"

The gambler renewed his struggles and increased the volume of the guttural noises he managed to utter.

"I think he's got a last request, Judge," said Harker, gloating.

"Let him talk."

The roustabout applying the brutal chokehold relaxed his arm.

"Judge," gasped Tyree, his voice shaking, "don't let them do it, for God's sakes! Don't let them murder me!"

"I call it justice," said Torn sternly.

"I'll make a deal."

"A bottom deal," muttered one of the roustabouts wryly.

"I'll listen," said Torn. "I like to think of myself as a reasonable man."

"If you'll let me live," said Tyree, "I'll give you Jack Jenkins."

CHAPTER 24

Torn's eyes narrowed into cold slits of gunmetal gray.

"How are you associated with Jenkins?" he asked the gambler.

"Do we have a deal?"

"I want to hear what you have to say."

A desperate calm overcame Tyree. He was fighting for his life. His voice was an earnest whisper. He was playing his last ace, and he knew he had to play it right or lose. "I could tell you what I know and then you might still hand me over to these"—Tyree prudently decided against using the derogatory term that came first to mind—"these gentlemen."

Torn nodded. "Mr. Harker, you and your men can go."

"But . . ."

"Let him go."

The crewmen were deeply disappointed. They were rough and rowdy characters, but not one of them seriously contemplated getting into a dispute with Torn. Something about the man opened their eyes to the wisdom of treading lightly in his presence.

"Let him be, boys," said Harker, dejected.

Tyree was released. He straightened collar and cuff, a tug here and a brush there. Torn thought he looked like a rooster in fancy plumage surrounded by a pack of shaggy wolves.

"What about the money we lost to him?" asked one of the roustabouts.

"Tyree," said Torn, "hand over your wallet."

"But I—"

"Our deal, if we make one, concerns whether you live or die. If you live, you're going to spend the first part of the rest of your life behind bars. You won't need money there."

Tyree had been holding on to a slender hope that he might win his release by giving up Jenkins. It could have worked out perfectly: Torn would have taken care of Jenkins, and Tyree would finally have been free from the ol' Corpse Maker, with no need to go through the rest of his life looking over his shoulder.

But the judge wasn't going to give him that much rope. Torn held all the cards. This was his deal. Tyree knew he had no choice but to play the game according to the dealer's rules.

So he surrendered his wallet. Harker snatched it out of his hand, checked the contents, and scowled.

"This might cover what a couple of us lost, Judge. But we got a half-dozen others in the crew who got cheated by this son of a bitch. What about them?"

"My God," said Torn, incredulous. "Tyree, you've

been playing with fire all along." He picked up the sample case and handed it to the first mate.

Harker looked inside. "What's this? Rocks?"

"High-grade ore samples. Silver."

Harker was dubious. "Looks like a bunch of rocks to me."

"I'm no expert," said Torn, "but I figure those 'rocks' will fetch a couple thousand dollars. I trust you to split whatever you get for them fairly among the men who lost at Tyree's table. That still may not be enough to compensate everyone fully. But then you should just chalk the rest up to an expensive lesson. Apparently it's a lesson every member of the crew needs to learn. I reckon most of you have families. Believe me, there are better ways to spend your wages than to risk them on the turn of a card."

Harker was getting over his disappointment. He grinned. "You're a fair man, Judge, and I guess we're getting a better shake than we deserve."

"You boys go on. I'll take care of Tyree."

The first mate herded the others out, pausing in the doorway. "If you need any help with Jenkins, Judge, I know I speak for all the men when I say you can count on us."

Torn was gratified. "There are a lot of men who would run from that name. Thanks."

With the *Sultana* men gone Torn grabbed a handful of Tyree's ruffled shirt and planted the gambler in a chair. He stood between Tyree and the door. "I asked this once before. This is the last time. How are you associated with Jenkins?"

"A few years ago, in New Orleans, I . . . became involved with the wife of a very influential and powerful man. He found out about his wife's infidelity. He was going to destroy me. But before he could, he disappeared. Some of Jenkins's men cut him up into little pieces and fed him to the gators."

"Why would Jenkins do that for you?"

"It wasn't for me. This man had been making trouble for Jenkins for a long time. You see, some of the less scrupulous merchants who do business in New Orleans had been buying stolen goods from Jenkins. This man had vowed to expose them. When Jenkins had the man disposed of, he killed two birds with one stone. He knew about my situation. He figured out a way to use it to his advantage. He made it clear I owed him."

"So you went to work for him."

"Don't you understand? I had no choice." Tyree explained how he selected rich victims for striker gangs to rob and murder.

"You ought to hang," said Torn.

"We had a deal!" cried the gambler.

"Yes. But I promise you, Tyree, you're going to spend a long time in jail."

"At least I'll be alive," said Tyree, his voice hollow. "If you kill Jenkins, that is. Once he's dead, the strikers will disband. No man could take Jenkins's place. No man could control the strikers."

"So where is he?"

"He's right here, aboard the *Sultana.*"

Tyree could see by the expression on Torn's face that the judge didn't believe him. "It's the truth, I swear it. He came aboard tonight. He's going to kill Sikes. He has fifty of his best men waiting upriver. They're going to come aboard, probably tomorrow night, and rob everyone. They're going to pick this boat clean."

"Jenkins, on board," murmured Torn. "Where?"

"You swear you'll keep your end of the—"

"Where?"

The stateroom door burst open.

Torn whirled.

A pistol barked. The hand lamp shattered, plunging the room into darkness. Torn dimly saw a shape move through the doorway. He swept the Colt Peacemaker up and fired. Something hit him just about as hard and fast as a freight train on a downhill run, knocking him clean off his feet. He nearly blacked out. Trying to get up, he realized he'd been pistol-whipped. Blood streamed down his face. A vicious kick caught him in the ribs, knocking the wind out of him. He heard Tyree shriek. A pistol spoke again.

Then Torn felt the barrel of a gun against the back of his neck.

He knew he was going to die.

A soft chuckle chilled him to the bone.

"This is too easy. Do try harder next time, Judge. I hate to be disappointed."

And then the man was gone, silent as a ghost.

Slowly, clumsily, Torn got to his feet. Reeling, he fetched up against a table. Making for the doorway, he tripped over Tyree's body and fell, cursing. Again he picked himself up—it took tremendous effort—and this time made it out onto the promenade. He collided with Harker. The first mate caught him and kept him from falling again.

"What happened?" asked Harker.

More crewmen were converging, drawn by the gunfire, coming from both ends of the promenade.

"You didn't see him?" asked Torn in disbelief.

"See who? I heard shots. I—"

"Damn," breathed Torn. "Come on."

He led the way, fighting to keep his balance, to the Kentucky stateroom.

The roustabout named Bledsoe was sprawled on the floor. He had been stabbed through the heart. His shirt was soaked with blood. Sikes was sitting in a chair, hands still bound, his head resting at an odd angle on one shoulder, eyes bulging, mouth gaping open in a silent scream.

"Holy Mother of God," gasped Harker.

Sikes's throat had been cut.

CHAPTER 25

AN HOUR LATER TORN STOOD IN CAPTAIN BLAKE'S QUARTERS, at the forward end of the texas deck. Duke Doniphan was present as well.

"Jack Jenkins on my ship," rasped Blake. "I don't believe it."

"You'd better," said Torn.

"You misunderstand me, sir. I hope he is. I can't believe I've been given such a golden opportunity."

Torn shook his head. The gleam in Blake's frosty blue eyes warned him that the man was more interested in the glory he would reap from being the man responsible for the capture of the most notorious criminal in the country than he was concerned for the welfare of his passengers and crew.

Torn had known men like Blake in the war, officers who sought renown at any cost. Almost inevitably they led their units to disaster. One who came to mind was George Armstrong Custer. Torn had fought the "Boy

General" on a number of occasions when he served with
Lee's Army of Northern Virginia and Custer had been
assigned to the Army of the Potomac. No one could
question Custer's courage and audacity, but courage
was no asset unless tempered with calm reason. The
casualties in Custer's command had been extremely
high. Recently the man had led his Seventh Cavalry into
a Sioux ambush at Little Bighorn. When Torn heard the
news, his first thought had been that Custer had finally
found the immortality he'd been seeking—at a terrible
cost.

Now Ezra Blake intended to lead the *Sultana* and everyone aboard her to another Little Bighorn. Torn
wasn't going to let that happen.

"We must get under way immediately," said Blake.
"We can't allow him to slip ashore. Doniphan—"

"You can't do that," said Torn.

Blake turned on him. "Keep in mind, sir, that this ship
is under my command. Doniphan, we will leave immediately."

"We can't, Captain, not at night. The river's too low
and the channel too tricky. We've got to wait until daylight."

Rage colored Blake's gaunt, bristly cheeks. "You will
do as I say."

"I most certainly will not," snapped the feisty pilot.
"Federal law prohibits me from obeying an order which
in my opinion jeopardizes the boat and everyone on
her."

"Federal law!" exploded Blake. "Why, you . . ."

He took a menacing step. Doniphan's hands curled
into fists. He tucked his chin. Torn stepped between
them.

"We've got a fight on our hands with Jenkins and his strikers. Save it for that. We don't have time for this. Doniphan is right, Captain, and you know it."

"You'll never work on the river again, Doniphan," declared Blake. "I am not without influence. People will listen to what I have to say."

"That's their problem," barked Doniphan.

"You can't change the routine," said Torn. "Jenkins will know something is wrong if we leave Vicksburg before sunrise."

Blake started pacing. "Jenkins must be captured. He killed one of my crewmen, and two others besides."

"I'm sorry about Bledsoe," said Torn. "But the others were Jenkins's own men. That just cuts down the odds against us."

"But why has he come aboard? Why is he taking such a chance."

"That's the kind of man he is. Robbing the *Sultana* will be his crowning achievement. It will guarantee him a place in the history books."

The one-armed skipper drew up short and stared at Torn. He understood what Torn was saying. He knew all about glory seeking. He'd lost an arm in the quest—and more men than he could count.

"He must know we are aware he is on the *Sultana*. Surely he fears being captured or killed."

"The only thing a man like Jenkins is afraid of is losing power. He has complete confidence in himself, in his ability to get out of any situation when it gets too hot. He's here to see with his own eyes what our reaction to what we know will be."

"Best thing to do, seems to me," said Doniphan, "is

let him know the game is up. Try to catch him, if we can. Any other way we risk the lives of everyone aboard."

Torn nodded grimly. "I've given it a lot of thought. But the fact is that Jenkins will try to carry out this scheme. If not on the *Sultana,* then on some other boat."

"You're assuming he'll get away."

"We can't take for granted that he won't. We have one chance, if we play our cards right, to put an end to Jenkins and the strikers."

"That's a dangerous game," said Doniphan.

"Yes, and one we've got to win."

"I will arm the crew," said Blake. "I have a few rifles, a half-dozen pistols, under lock and key."

"He would expect you to," replied Torn. "And I think we should question every man aboard we do not personally know."

"But wouldn't that . . . ?"

"Again, he would expect it. If we do nothing, if we act as though nothing is wrong, he will smell a rat. The reason we must continue upriver is to make the rendezvous with the strikers."

"If this man is as clever as you think," said Blake, "how can you hope he will give himself away?"

"I don't. But we've got to appear to be doing something."

"I take it you've got some kind of plan to deal with the strikers," said Doniphan.

"I do. You'll have to work with me, Duke."

"You're forgetting I am the captain of this ship," said Blake frostily.

"If we get Jenkins, you can have all the credit," replied Torn. "And the only chance you have of getting him is to do as I say."

Blake glowered, but made no further comment.

CHAPTER 26

TORN WENT BACK TO HIS STATEROOM TO GET SOME SLEEP. SUN-rise was only a few hours away. He had a hunch tomorrow would be one hell of a day.

The bodies of Sikes and Bledsoe had been removed. The chair Sikes had been sitting in when his throat had been cut was gone. A cabin boy was going after the blood stains on the floor with a brush and soapy water. Harker arrived a few minutes later to ask Torn if he wanted another room. Torn declined. All he wanted was sleep.

Harker was envious. "I could use some shut-eye, too, Judge. But I don't think I'll get a wink as long as I know Jack Jenkins is aboard."

The first mate left, taking the cabin boy with him. In spite of all the cleaning up, the smell of death lingered. It didn't bother Torn. He wouldn't let it. He had spent many a night on the blood-soaked ground of a battlefield, waiting for tomorrow's fight. This was no different.

He took off his coat and stretched out on the bed, the saber-knife still strapped to his side, the Colt Peacemaker in his hand.

Doubts kept swirling in his mind. He realized full well that he was risking the lives of all on board the riverboat. To deal with that realization he had to remind himself that as long as Jack Jenkins and his strikers were in operation, no one on the river was safe. He looked at that from every angle and convinced himself it was a valid point. Jenkins had to be stopped, at all costs.

He had something else to deal with. Fear.

This is too easy. Do try harder next time, Judge.

He had to admit to himself that he was afraid of Jack Jenkins.

Witnessing the man's handiwork tonight, he had seen fully and at first hand what kind of foe he was up against. Jenkins was a born killer. Corpse Maker, indeed. He was bold, ruthless, and utterly without conscience. He was more than a match for Torn physically. And he was brilliant, in an evil way. Most chilling of all was the supreme confidence he had displayed in letting Torn live.

Torn's own confidence was shaken. Rarely had he crossed swords with a man he knew he could not outfight or outwit. This time, with Jenkins, he wasn't too sure.

He thought about Karl Schmidt, the sergeant at the federal prison camp of Point Lookout, Maryland, where Torn had been incarcerated for the last sixteen months of the war. Schmidt had been a sadist, and he had made destroying Torn his first priority. To a degree Torn had been afraid of Schmidt. It was unreasonable to expect a man who found himself at the mercy of a sadist not to be afraid. But all along Torn had held firm to his conviction that sooner or later Schmidt would make a mistake.

The difference with Jenkins was that the ol' Corpse Maker didn't make mistakes.

Torn grimly pushed all the doubts out of his mind, turned over on his side, and went to sleep, finger on the trigger of the Colt, thumb on the hammer.

He awoke with a start, to an insistent tapping on the stateroom door. It was a cabin boy, whose eyes got big as saucers when he saw the Colt Peacemaker. Mollified, Torn put the gun behind his back.

"Sorry, boy. I had a bad night."

"Yes, sir." The youngster gulped. "Mr. Ashbrook would like to see you, sir."

Torn sighed. "Tell him I'll be along."

"He says he will wait for you in the dining room."

Torn closed the door, listened to the boy's bare feet slapping the deck as he scampered down the promenade like his pants were on fire.

Torn took the time to make himself presentable. He shaved and tried to get the blood out of his hair—the scalp wound he had received last night, courtesy of Jack Jenkins, had opened up while he slept, tossing and turning fitfully. He put on a clean shirt.

There was no point in trying to fool himself, so he didn't try. He wanted Rebecca Ashbrook's last impression of him to be a good one.

He found the Ashbrooks at a table in the ornate dining room. Ashbrook had ordered a hearty breakfast, but hadn't done much more than pick at his food. He was clearly agitated. There were dark circles under his eyes. Rebecca looked as lovely and serene as ever. Her smile was a little sad, as though she knew what was coming. Her gaze was warm and trusting, and Torn knew, without any words passing between them, that she had already forgiven him for what he had to do. Somehow that didn't make it any easier.

A white-coated steward appeared to take Torn's order. Torn sent him away.

"I heard shooting last night," said Ashbrook. "This morning I overheard a crewman say Tyree was dead. Did you . . . ?"

"He's dead all right."

Ashbrook was relieved. "Daughter, we're safe."

"You still have me to worry about," said Torn.

"I was hoping, sir, for old times' sake, at least, that you—"

"Whether you ever knew my father or not is of no consequence," snapped Torn.

"I see." Ashbrook turned a violent shade of red. "I was hoping we could settle our differences like gentlemen. Clearly I was mistaken."

Ashbrook's indignant tone rubbed Torn the wrong way. "You're a swindler, Ashbrook, and I ought to put you behind bars."

Ashbrook looked to Rebecca for help. She made no comment, and Ashbrook, realizing she would not rush to his defense this time, dropped the indignant act and seemed to fall apart. He put his head in his hands and sobbed quietly.

"Pull yourself together," said Torn in a fierce whisper.

"Oh God, what have I done!"

Rebecca put a hand on her father's arm. The look she gave Torn was a silent plea for mercy.

"You're not going to jail, Ashbrook," said Torn, relenting. "You're going back to Mexico. And you're going to stay there."

"Yes. Yes." Ashbrook composed himself. "Please try to understand. What I did, I did for my daughter's sake. I . . . I have always felt as though I had failed her. I wanted to leave her *something.*"

"Father, all I ever wanted or needed was your love."

Ashbrook squeezed her hand. "It wasn't for myself," he told Torn. "Please believe that."

"I do," said Torn, his voice hollow.

"What of the samples?"

"You don't need them. Your swindling days are over."

The *Sultana*'s steam whistle shrilled three times.

Torn drew a long breath. "We'll be leaving Vicksburg in a half hour. You'll be going in the other direction."

"Yes. Well. Come, Rebecca. We must pack our belongings. Time is short."

"I'll be along, Father."

Standing, Ashbrook looked from her to Torn and back again. He opened his mouth to speak, but the words didn't come. Crestfallen, he walked away.

Watching him go, Torn felt sorry—sorry for John Raleigh Ashbrook, a man who carried self-imposed guilt for failing to provide his daughter with the material things he thought she ought to have; for Rebecca, whose father did not comprehend that all he had to give her was his love; and for himself, though least of all.

He looked at Rebecca, though it hurt to do so, for he knew that it would be the last time he would see her.

"I'm sorry," she said.

"For what?"

She hesitated, picking her words with care. "I sense it might have turned out differently, in another time and place."

Torn was surprised. She had articulated exactly what he was feeling.

"I don't suppose you ever get down to Mexico," she said, in a lighter tone of voice that seemed just a little strained.

"Who knows?"

"Yes. Who knows what tomorrow might bring? But today . . . today I have to help my father. He needs me to be with him. He's afraid. Afraid I'll leave him. I am all he has left."

Torn nodded, experiencing a miserable emptiness, sensing that a rare chance for happiness was about to pass him by, and knowing he was powerless to prevent it from passing. "We all have responsibilities," he said, thinking about Melony Hancock.

Until he found Melony, or found out what had become of her, he would always have to let the chances pass him by.

They sat there in silence for a moment, until a steward arrived to remind them that all those who wished to disembark should do so immediately.

Torn didn't let him finish. "We know," he snapped, and the steward beat a hasty retreat.

Rebecca put her hand on his and whispered, "Good-bye."

He did not watch her go; instead he took the daguerreotype of Melony out of his pocket and sat there staring at it until he felt the big side-wheels start to turn, moving the riverboat out into the main channel.

CHAPTER 27

"I WANT TO EXPLAIN," SAID CAPTAIN BLAKE, "THAT I AM QUESTIONING every man aboard this vessel in the course of an inquiry into three killings which occurred last night. I have interviewed a dozen before you and have told them precisely the same thing. I say this because I do not wish for you to think you are being singled out for any reason, Mister . . ."

"Jones. Nathaniel Jones. Mos' folks call me Natty."

As he spoke Jack Jenkins glanced across Blake's quarters at Torn, who stood leaning against the wall near the door, arms folded across his chest, ankles crossed as well. Torn appeared only politely curious. His posture was not at all threatening. But Jenkins knew that Torn was a lot more interested in these proceedings than he made out to be. A ghost of a smile touched the corner of the Corpse Maker's mouth. Neither Torn nor Blake detected the smile beneath the scraggly, tobacco-stained beard Jenkins had adopted for the role of Natty Jones, crusty old rebel warrior.

"Mr. Jones, then," said Blake, nodding. His one arm rested on a small rolltop desk. His chair was turned at an angle so that he could face Jenkins, who sat in another chair beside the desk. "I take it by the clothes you wear that you served in the Confederate army."

Jenkins gave Blake a suspicious, sidelong squint. "And I hear tell you was on the other side of that little dustup. Now you ain't gonna hold that agin me, are you, Captain?"

"Of course not. The war is over."

"True enough, though it still pains me some to admit it. There was just too damn many of you Billy Yanks, and that's a cold fact."

Blake forced a polite smile. "Let's get to the business at hand. Did you see anything out of the ordinary last night, Mr. Jones?"

Jenkins tugged on his beard a moment, in an attitude of intense thought, and finally shook his head. "Nope. Can't say as I did. I heard shots fired. Raised a commotion down on the main deck. Two shots, as I recollect."

"I believe there were three."

Jenkins shrugged. "Three, then. I was asleep; the commotion woke me up. When I didn't hear no more shootin', I just rolled over and proceeded to get some more shut-eye. Man's gotta get his rest, I always say. Fact is, during the war, the boys said I could sleep right through Armageddon. They had to wake me up for the charge on Seminary Ridge. Slept right through the artillery barrage."

"You were at Gettysburg?"

"Lost a few friends that day," said Jenkins ruefully.

"Where are you bound?"

"Sent Looey. Look up an ol' feller who was in my company."

"Are you armed, Mr. Jones?"

"Is rain wet?" Jenkins reached under his butternut-gray tunic and brandished an old Griswold cap-and-ball pistol. "She ain't much to look at, but she's reliable." He squinted again. "Why do you ask?"

"Just curious."

"Curious, huh?" Jenkins snorted. "You think maybe I killed whoever it was got killed. Thing is, I don't even know who that was. Heard talk it was a tinhorn gambler. But I don't know anybody on this bucket, so why would I do it? What happened, anyhow?"

"A man named Tyree was shot and killed. You heard right—he was a gambler. Also, one of my roustabouts was murdered, and another passenger named Sikes."

"Well, I'll be. It was a big night for bloodlettin', weren't it?" Jenkins shoved the Griswold back under his tunic. "Better keep her close by. Don't want you to be sittin' there tomorrow asking everybody if they had any reason to kill me."

"We don't expect any further trouble," said Blake, "but we're taking certain precautions."

"Yeah, I seen some of your crew walkin' around with thumb busters and long guns."

"There is a killer aboard, Mr. Jones."

"Got a notion as to why all these pilgrims got sent to Saint Peter?"

"Money, probably," replied Blake. "Tyree was known to carry large sums."

"You can search me. I got about four dollars on me and some change, not counting a roll of Dixie shinplasters." Jenkins grinned. "Hell, I don't know why I hold on to 'em. Guess maybe I'm waiting for the South to rise again."

"I would hope," said Blake stiffly, "that you Southerners learned from your mistakes."

Torn sensed it was time for him to intervene. Blake had been doing fine until now. The *Sultana's* skipper was letting old grudges get in the way. "The war is over, gentlemen. Remember?"

"Quite right," said Blake. "Thank you, Mr. Jones. I hope we can get you to your destination without further inconvenience."

"If your killer decides to try and add me to his list, I'll inconvenience him something fierce." Jenkins stood. "I'm happy to oblige, Captain."

Torn waited until Jenkins reached the door before asking, "What was your regiment, Mr. Jones?"

China-blue eyes squinted suspiciously. Torn's posture was still casual. His arms were still folded across his chest, and Jenkins was confident he could react faster than Torn could draw the Colt Peacemaker in the holster on his hip. The question was offhand, seemingly without special significance. It was a query one might expect one veteran to ask another. Reviewing what had been said since his arrival in Blake's quarters, Jenkins decided there was no reason to think he had been found out. So he took Torn's question at face value.

"Sixth Mississippi. You?"

"First South Carolina Cavalry."

Jenkins winked and thumbed over his shoulder at Ezra Blake. "Still say we could have whupped 'em if there hadn't been so danged many."

Torn smiled and shrugged. "Have a nice day, Mr. Jones."

Jenkins nodded, opened the door. As he stepped across the threshold he saw Torn's arms unfold. He crouched, turned, and reached for the Griswold at the same time, fast as a rattler could strike. But Torn was faster. He'd had his right hand under the frock coat, gripping the saber-knife all along. The leather thong that held the weapon upside down in the sheath had been removed.

He bulled into Jenkins, knocking him off balance, slamming the saber-knife's single-guard bow down on Jenkins's head. With a grunt Jenkins dropped, but he didn't black out, and he was still trying to bring the Griswold into action. Torn's well-placed kick struck the revolver out of his grasp, sent it skittering down the hallway. Torn struck again with the saber-knife. Jenkins threw out an arm and warded off the blow. He grabbed Torn's leg with the other hand and pulled it out from under him. Torn landed hard, and before he knew it, Jenkins was swarming all over him. Jenkins grabbed his right wrist and kept the saber-knife away. He reached for the Colt in Torn's holster with his left. Torn put everything he had into a punch that snapped Jenkins's head back and rocked him off balance. Driving a knee into Jenkins's side, he got the man off him and bounced to his feet. Jenkins was up quickly as well. Tossing the saber-knife from right hand to left, Torn drew the Colt and aimed at a spot between those china-blue eyes.

Jenkins froze.

Then he chuckled. "You did a lot better this time, Judge."

"Live or die, it's up to you."

Jenkins looked right down the barrel of the Peace-maker and grinned. "You won't take me alive."

He lunged at Torn.

Torn didn't pull the trigger. Instead he sidestepped and clubbed Jenkins with the barrel of the Colt.

Jenkins sprawled, out cold.

Torn looked across at Blake. Everything had happened so quickly that the *Sultana*'s captain hadn't moved—was still standing over by the rolltop desk, looking nonplussed.

"He finally made a mistake," said Torn.

"What are you talking about? You mean Jones?"

"This is Jack Jenkins."

Blake stared at the unconscious man. "How can you be sure?"

"The Sixth Mississippi wasn't at Gettysburg."

"You know that for a fact?"

"I was with the Army of Northern Virginia from Second Manassas to Gettysburg. I'm sure. But Jenkins didn't fight in the war. He was too busy robbing and killing all up and down this river. So he had to do some guessing. And he guessed wrong."

Blake was silent a moment, still staring at Jenkins. "Why didn't you kill him?"

Torn drew a ragged breath. He had been asking himself that same question.

"He's too dangerous to let live," added Blake.

Torn shook his head. "I've never shot an unarmed man. I won't. I don't care who it is."

"Good God, man, this is Jack Jenkins."

"Every man gets a fair chance with me. Jenkins could have killed me last night, but he didn't."

Blake switched his stare to Torn. He looked at Torn

as he might look at a lunatic. "Fair play?" he rasped. "Fair chance? You can't give Jenkins any chance at all."

Torn grimaced. Blake was scared of Jack Jenkins. Everybody on the river who had any sense at all was scared of the Corpse Maker. Torn knew how the captain felt. But he wasn't going to do something that went against the grain just because he was afraid.

"So what do you have in mind, Captain?" he asked. "You want me to put a bullet in the back of his head?"

"It occurred to me," said Blake.

"No. That won't happen."

Blake turned away, disgusted. He began to pace feverishly.

"It isn't over yet," said Torn. "I need your help, Captain. This is war, and I need all the good soldiers I can find."

"You're patronizing me."

"I don't do that."

Blake paced for a moment, grimly silent. Torn waited patiently.

"Very well." Blake sighed. "What would you have me do?"

"I'll need ten volunteers. Ten brave men. Everyone else gets off at the next stop."

"What are you planning?"

"Jenkins's strikers are waiting upriver to ambush this boat. I don't want to keep them waiting."

CHAPTER 28

THE DAY, IT SEEMED TO TORN, WOULD NEVER END.

They discharged all the passengers at Greenville. There were some who did not care to be inconvenienced in this manner, but when they were told that the *Sultana* might be the target of Jack Jenkins's strikers, their reluctance disappeared.

As for volunteers, Torn had more than he needed. Almost the entire crew, save for the cabin boys and stewards, offered to stick with him. Torn was gratified, but it presented him with difficult decisions—those he picked would likely lose their lives.

The decision was made a little easier by eliminating those who were married and had families. In the end Torn had the first mate, Harker, seven roustabouts, Duke Doniphan, and the red-haired giant named Quinn.

"I don't need two pilots," Torn told Quinn.

"There's never been but one pilot on this bucket,"

replied Quinn, wearing a stubborn scowl. "And that's yours truly."

Torn repressed a smile. "Are you married?"

"Yep. Married to this damn river ever since I was knee-high to an alligator."

"Well, I—"

"Look," rasped Quinn, exasperated, "is there gonna be a fight or not?"

"I expect so."

"Then by God I'm going with you," growled Quinn. "I come from a long line of iron-jawed, brass-mounted, copper-bellied skull busters. So if there's gonna be a ruckus up ahead, I aim to be present, and I will be if I have to swim the rest of the way. That's my final word on the matter."

So Quinn went along.

Captain Blake was another problem. He did not think it proper to leave his ship in the hands of others. Torn put Jenkins in his custody.

"You could just hand him over to the Greenville sheriff," said Blake.

"No. I don't know the Greenville sheriff. But I know you, Captain. And you're the only man I can trust with my prisoner."

Blake suspiciously studied Torn's face. "What's your game, Judge?"

"No games. I mean what I say." Torn stuck out his hand.

Surprised, Blake shook it. "I guess maybe the war *is* over," he said.

Not a minute was wasted at Greenville. By midafternoon the *Sultana* was plowing upriver. Torn and the two pilots stayed in the pilothouse while Harker and the others kept the boilers fed for full steam.

Quinn manned the wheel. Doniphan unfolded a chart depicting in detail the river ahead. He pointed out a few things to Torn.

"Ordinarily, I'd say these charts aren't worth the trouble it took to make them. I don't know why they call the Mississippi the Father of Waters, 'cause in my opinion she's as fickle as a woman. Always changing. Full of surprises, and most of them damned unpleasant. For instance, here. Hat Island. Well, Hat Island is gone. Nothing left of Hat Island except bad memories. Only way to know what lies ahead is to talk to other pilots. You talk to the ones who've come downriver when you're going up, and those going up when you're coming down. Problem is, there aren't that many riverboats in business anymore, and too few good pilots. Hard times."

"So where do you think they'll ambush us?"

Doniphan shrugged, studying the chart. "We're about on schedule. They'd figure us to be right along here by the end of the day, and we'll be there if we keep working Harker and his boys to death on the boilers. Think it'll be at night?"

Torn nodded. "I sure hope so. In full daylight they'd be able to see something was wrong—that there weren't enough folks aboard. Where would you lay up for the night?"

"Here, at the foot of Island Thirty-seven. No towns, no wharf boats on this stretch. And we wouldn't run the Chain at night."

"The Chain?"

"On the east side of the island, where the channel

lies. Sunken rocks. And the skeletons of eighteen riverboats."

"Those are just the ones you sunk, right?" asked Quinn.

"If I wasn't saving myself for the big fight, I'd whup you to a thin frazzle, Quinn."

Quinn guffawed. "You couldn't whup a one-legged dog, Doniphan."

Torn smiled. "Okay, gentlemen."

"The Chain is a bad place, all right," said Doniphan. "One of the worst. Bad as Hanging Dog, and the Graveyard at Goose Island. Calculate at this rate we'll make Island Thirty-seven by sunset."

The afternoon dragged by. Torn went down to the boilers and made sure Harker and the roustabouts knew what they were supposed to do. Every man had a rifle and a revolver. They were quiet, and Torn knew they were scared. That was all right. He wouldn't have trusted them if they hadn't been a little apprehensive. He could see the grim resolve in their expressions and knew also that they would fight well. The Mississippi did not breed too many cowards.

Back in the pilothouse Torn watched the wooded banks and steep bluffs slip by. He saw an occasional cabin in a clearing. On the western shore the forests were interspersed with vast canebrakes. He wondered if Jenkins's camp was nearby. He wondered, too, if it was true what Sikes had said, that if Jenkins was gone, the strikers would disband.

He tried not to check his Ingersoll too often. The eve of battle was worse than the battle itself. He speculated about his own survival, just as he had done before Antietam, and Chancellorsville, and Gettysburg. Then he thought about Melony, and the long years of futile searching, always confronted by the cold reality that he would probably never see her again, and he thought about Rebecca Ashbrook, and missed chances, and he was one step shy of not really caring too much about survival by the time Island Thirty-seven hove into view. It wasn't that hard to die when you didn't have much to live for.

Island Thirty-seven was thickly wooded, about three quarters of a mile long and two hundred yards wide. The river was narrow here, and bending gradually. On the western shore was a marsh. Quinn eased the riverboat up to the southern tip of the island, pretty as you please. Two roustabouts used long ropes with grappling hooks to warp the *Sultana* to a pair of stout trees. Torn used the speaking tube to issue a curt order to Harker down in the engine room.

"Stoke 'em."

The sun was setting, a fireball sinking slowly into the marsh, turning the surface of the mighty river red as blood.

Duke Doniphan broke out his spyglass, and Torn advised him to watch the western shore.

"How do you know they'll come from that direction?" asked the pilot.

"They'll put the sun behind them and in our eyes, if they plan to come soon."

"They could wait until late at night."

"They've been waiting a long time. If they're here, they'll come soon."

The next quarter hour was an eternity. Torn listened to the murmur of the river as it swept past the riverboat. He heard gators grunting from the banks of Island

Thirty-seven, and off in the distance the eerie cry of a loon.

Harker came bounding up the pilothouse guy. "If we don't open the steam valves, those boilers will blow us to kingdom come," he warned Torn.

"Wait a little while longer," said Torn, with a steely calm.

Doniphan lowered the spyglass, rubbed his eyes, and then resumed scanning the marsh. Only the tip of the sun remained above the broken horizon.

"We're sitting on a damned powder keg, Judge," whispered Harker.

"Wait," said Torn.

Doniphan tensed. Torn saw it, and his heart began to pound against his rib cage.

"My God," breathed the pilot. "Here they come."

Torn took the spyglass to see for himself.

He counted eight small boats, coming out of the marsh grass, gliding across the river in the murky gloom of the gray twilight.

CHAPTER 29

"TEN MINUTES," CALCULATED DONIPHAN, HIS VOICE AS TAUT AS new-strung barbed wire. He turned to Harker. "How long before . . . ?"

He didn't finish the sentence. Didn't have to. Everyone in the pilothouse knew exactly what he was referring to.

"How do I know?" asked the first mate. "I can tell you one thing, though. I'd rather not hang around to find out."

There was no way to know precisely how long the boilers, fully stoked and with the valves that released the steam pressure closed off, would hold up. When one exploded, the other seven would go as well. It would be like eight bombs detonating at once, ripping the riverboat open. The blast would kill everyone aboard.

Torn was aware of this—aware that any second the boilers would blow. Any second might be his last on earth. But he focused on the job at hand. "Harker, get all your men to their positions on the main deck. Make sure the sounding boat is secure on the starboard side. And remember, no one starts shooting until I do."

The first mate gave Torn that knuckle salute and hastened down the pilothouse guy.

Torn returned the spyglass to Doniphan. He'd brought his valise up to the pilothouse; now he drew the Winchester 44/40 out of the scabbard strapped to the side of the valise. He didn't have to check to make sure it was loaded.

"A hundred yards," said Doniphan.

The sun was gone, but the last shreds of daylight yet streaked the sky. The surface of the river, no longer bloodred, was now a kaleidoscope of silver and indigo. Torn's eyes were keen; he could still make out most of the boats.

They've got to be wondering what's going on, he thought. Wondering why the *Sultana* is so dark and quiet. Fearing that it might be a trap.

But they were still coming on, the boats lined up. He could see the flash of foam as oars bit deep into the water.

"Time to give them an invitation they can't refuse," he muttered.

He smashed one of the big windows on the port side of the pilothouse with the stock of the Winchester. As the glass shattered and rained down he swept the repeater to his shoulder and began firing as fast as he could work the action. A sudden, relentless calm swept over him.

The waiting was over. The fight was on.

Quinn smashed another window. He and Doniphan began shooting. They both had sideguns, and the range was too great for them to be effective, but Torn didn't object.

Down below, on the main deck, Harker and the roustabouts joined in. Gun thunder rolled across the river. The strikers responded. Muzzleflash blossomed from dozens of guns. Bullets peppered the pilothouse, smashing the rest of the windows, splintering the walls. Torn crouched, balanced the barrel of the Winchester on the window sash, and kept firing until the long gun was empty. Then, with cool deliberation, he returned it to its scabbard and drew the Colt. Glancing across the pilothouse, he noticed that Doniphan and Quinn had hit the floor.

"Damned good shots," muttered Doniphan, shaken.

"They like to fight," said Torn.

He smiled.

Doniphan saw this, and was awed by it. Those bastards are turning this boat into so much kindling, he thought, and we're a short hair away from a dying and this man is grinning like a hungry loafer wolf.

And then he thought, Thank God he's on our side.

"We got their blood up," said Torn, exultant. "No chance they'll turn back now."

The strikers were responding exactly as he had hoped. He had dealt with men like this enough to know how they thought. Like coyotes, they'd turn tail and run if they smelled a trap. But if you nipped their heels, they'd turn and fight.

"Time to go," he said.

He headed for the door.

"Don't have to tell me twice," said Doniphan, scrambling to his feet to follow. "Come on, Quinn. This ain't the time to take a nap."

But Quinn, facedown on the floor, didn't move.

Torn rolled him over gently. Saw the blood, the bullet holes.

"No," breathed Doniphan, stunned, standing there oblivious to the swarm of hot lead.

Torn grabbed him by the arm and dragged him down. "He's dead. Shot through the heart."

Grief wrenched at Doniphan's features. "I never told him. . . ."

"That you counted him a friend," said Torn. "He knew. Now come on."

"I'll be seeing you, Quinn," murmured Doniphan. "You were a lightning pilot, all right."

Torn led the way down the pilothouse guy. He felt a bullet tug at his coattails. Doniphan grunted in pain and pitched forward into him, knocking him off balance. He caught himself, turned, and kept the pilot from tumbling the rest of the way.

"Where are you hit?"

"Leg," gasped Doniphan through clenched teeth.

Torn draped him over his left shoulder and carried him the rest of the way. He paused at the port-side railing of the hurricane deck. Directly below him the strikers were swarming onto the main deck. Harker and the roustabouts were pulling back, using the stacks of cordwood and freight on the main deck for cover. Torn fired twice. One striker sprawled dead. Another was hurled backward into the river. Before the other strikers could respond, Torn was gone.

At the starboard railing Torn could look down and see Harker and his men, firing back across the open main deck at the steadily advancing strikers.

The sounding boat was tied fast to the main-deck railing, the current bumping it against the riverboat's hull.

"You'll have to jump for it," he told Doniphan.

"Just put me down and watch me."

It wasn't a long drop, but Doniphan landed poorly. Harker looked up and yelled something. Torn couldn't make it out above the din of gunfire. He climbed over the railing and jumped, landing with the agility of a cat.

"Get in the boat," he told Harker.

Bellowing at the top of his lungs, Harker relayed the order to the other roustabouts, who were falling back to the sounding boat. Torn took a quick head count. There were five crewmen left, and he didn't need to ask about the others. Before he had finished counting, one of the five dropped, shot dead.

The remaining roustabouts clambered into the sounding boat. Harker assisted Doniphan, and Torn tried to cover them, emptying the Colt Peacemaker at the strikers swarming across the main deck.

"Come on!" yelled Harker.

As Torn turned he saw Hannibal.

The mulatto was coming straight for him, cane knife raised high.

Torn holstered the empty Colt and drew the saber-knife. He slashed the line that attached the sounding boat to the railing. The current was quick to sweep the sounding boat away from the *Sultana*.

Harker was yelling at him to jump, but Torn wasn't listening.

"Unfinished business," he said, and whirled to meet Hannibal's charge.

CHAPTER

30

THE THOUGHT FOREMOST IN TORN'S MIND WAS THAT HANNIBAL was too dangerous to let live.

True, the *Sultana* was going to go up in a great big blazing ball of flame any second, and it would probably kill everyone aboard. But you couldn't take chances with a man like Hannibal. Torn was willing to sacrifice his own life just to make sure the mulatto never came at anybody again with that cane knife raised overhead.

Hannibal was running as fast as he could, expecting Torn to go over the railing into the sounding boat and wanting to close the distance between them before that happened. When Torn squared off with the saber-knife in hand, the mulatto's eyes blazed with fierce elation.

There were several strikers on Hannibal's heels. The mulatto pulled up short and threw his arms out. "He's mine!" he roared, and the strikers stopped.

Dropping into a crouch, Hannibal moved in slowly,

flipping the cane knife from one hand to the other. "I said we'd fight again," he snarled.

Torn didn't waste his breath on a reply. He watched Hannibal's eyes. He saw them widen slightly a split second before the mulatto lunged and brought the cane knife down in a vicious blow that would have split Torn from skull to scrotum had he not been as quick and lithe as a cat. Hannibal put such force behind the swing that he seemed to lose his balance and stumble forward. Torn almost took the bait—almost slipped in to strike with the saber-knife. But then he realized that Hannibal was wielding his blade like a rank amateur. And Torn knew that wasn't so. He jumped back—just in time. The mulatto brought the cane knife up in a stroke that missed gutting Torn by a short inch. Torn feinted with the saber-knife and threw a left hook that caught Hannibal squarely on the chin. Hannibal's head snapped back. He staggered, but did not fall. The cane knife came sweeping down again. Torn parried with the saber-knife. Steel rang against steel. Sparks flew. Torn threw another left. Like the first this one connected solidly. Hannibal laughed and spat blood. He tried to run Torn through with the cane knife. Torn deflected the thrust. Hannibal plowed into him, driving him back against the railing. Torn gasped as the top rail caught him in the small of the back. Hannibal's weight bent him backward. Torn drove the saber-knife into the mulatto's side. Hannibal roared in pain and rage. Torn wedged a forearm under the man's chin and pressed against the windpipe, forcing Hannibal backward. Then he turned the saber-knife and ripped the mulatto's belly open. Hannibal jackknifed. The cane knife clattered on the bloody deck. Torn wrenched the saber-knife free. Hannibal dropped to his knees, slowly raised his head.

"You fight good," he mumbled, drooling blood.

Then he pitched forward on his face.

"Kill him!" yelled a striker.

Torn whirled and vaulted over the railing. Guns spoke. And then the guns were drowned out by a much larger noise as the *Sultana*'s boilers exploded.

The blast hurled Torn thirty feet. He blacked out in midair, but the shock of the cold water as he pinwheeled into the river brought him to. Stunned, he sank like a rock, began to lose consciousness again. His lungs ached for want of air. He started to inhale. When the water entered his lungs, he snapped wide-awake, panicked, and began to flail for the surface. All he could see was inky blackness. He was vomiting water and trying to keep from drawing more in at the same time. He couldn't make it. He was going to die. And just as he accepted that fact he broke the surface.

There was a lot of floating debris. Some of it was burning. In the hellish glow of these fires Torn saw the head and torso of one of the strikers drift by on the current. The arms and legs had been ripped off by the explosion, and the rest was a bloody, mangled mess.

The *Sultana* was gone.

Gasping for air, Torn saw part of the big pilot's wheel floating past. He swam to it, held on for dear life, and let it carry him downriver.

A few minutes later the men in the sounding boat found him and pulled him aboard.

"Be careful with that fancy pigsticker, Judge," said Harker. "We're a little crowded here, and you might hurt somebody."

Only then did Torn become aware that he was still clutching the saber-knife.

They floated downriver until dawn, and then put to shore on the Tennessee side.

One of the roustabouts had been gut-shot. When they laid him out on the ground, they discovered he had died during the night. Two others were wounded. The rest were exhausted. They stretched out on the bank, too weary to even fight the swarm of mosquitoes that descended upon them.

About midmorning Torn heard riders coming. It turned out to be Captain Blake, accompanied by the Greenville sheriff and a half-dozen heavily armed men.

"My God," breathed Blake. "You're alive."

"Just barely, some of us," replied Torn. He looked across at Duke Doniphan. The pilot had gone into shock. Torn had applied a makeshift field dressing to the gunshot wound in Doniphan's leg and covered the man with his tattered frock coat. "We've got three men who need a doctor. Quick."

"There's a town a few miles east," said the sheriff, and he dispatched one of his deputies to fetch a wagon and a sawbones.

"My ship . . ." said Blake.

"Gone," said Torn. "And the strikers went down with her. Jenkins and his bunch are finished."

"Jenkins is dead."

"What?"

The sheriff looked sheepish. "He tried to break out of my jail last night, Judge. We chased him down to the river. He had a gun. Took it from one of my deputies.

After he broke his neck. We traded lead. I know I hit him at least twice in the chest. He fell into the river."

"You're certain he's dead."

The sheriff nodded. "I'm sure."

Without another word Torn walked down to the edge of the river. He sat on his heels and watched the mighty Mississippi roll by. None of the others bothered him. They could sense he wished to be alone.

He tried to convince himself that the sheriff was right —that Jack Jenkins was dead. The ol' Corpse Maker was a corpse. Still, he couldn't rid himself of a gnawing doubt. Something about Jenkins . . .

It just seemed too easy.

But if it was true, it was poetic justice; Jack Jenkins at the bottom of the Mississippi, the very river to which he had committed the bodies of who knew how many victims.

Across the river, in Arkansas, stood a stretch of canebrake. Torn watched it for a long time. Finally he stood, stiff and sore, and turned away from the river. He thought he heard a soft and sinister chuckle above the song of the river. But no, it was just his imagination.

He walked on.

Saddle-up to these

THE REGULATOR *by Dale Colter*
Sam Slater, blood brother of the Apache
and a cunning bounty-hunter, is out to
collect the big price on the heads of the
murderous Pauley gang. He'll give them
a single choice: surrender and live, or go
for your sixgun.

THE REGULATOR—Diablo At Daybreak
by Dale Colter
The Governor wants the blood of the
Apache murderers who ravaged his
daughter. He gives Sam Slater a choice:
work for him, or face a noose. Now
Slater must hunt down the deadly rene-
gade Chacon...Slater's Apache brother.

THE JUDGE *by Hank Edwards*
Federal Judge Clay Torn is more than a
judge—sometimes he has to be the jury
and the executioner. Torn pits himself
against the most violent and ruthless
man in Kansas, a battle whose final verdict will judge one man right...and one
man dead.

THE JUDGE—War Clouds
by Hank Edwards
Judge Clay Torn rides into Dakota where
the Cheyenne are painting for war and
the army is shining steel and loading
lead. If war breaks out, someone is
going to make a pile of money on a river
of blood.

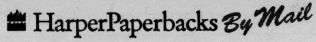

If you would like to receive a HarperPaperbacks
catalog, fill out the coupon below and send $1.00
postage/handling to:

HarperPaperbacks Catalog Request
10 East 53rd St.
New York, NY 10022

Name _____

Address _____

State _____ Zip _____